DOVER · THRIFT · EDITIONS

Hamlet

WILLIAM SHAKESPEARE

DOVER PUBLICATIONS, INC.
New York

DOVER THRIFT EDITIONS

General Editor: Stanley Appelbaum
Editor of This Volume: Shane Weller

Performance

This Dover Thrift Edition may be used in its entirety, in adaptation or in any other way for theatrical productions, professional and amateur, in the United States, without fee, permission or acknowledgment. (This may not apply outside of the United States, as copyright conditions may vary.)

This Dover edition, first published in 1992, contains the unabridged text of *Hamlet* as published in Volume VII of the second edition of *The Works of William Shakespeare*, Macmillan and Co., London, 1892. The Note and explanatory footnotes were prepared specially for the present edition. Additional information on the text reprinted here is given in the Note.

Manufactured in the United States of America
Dover Publications, Inc., 31 East 2nd Street, Mineola, N.Y. 11501

Library of Congress Cataloging-in-Publication Data

Shakespeare, William, 1564–1616.
Hamlet / William Shakespeare.
p. cm. — (Dover thrift editions)
"Contains the unabridged text of Hamlet as published in volume VII of the second edition of The works of William Shakespeare, Macmillan and Co., London, 1892"—T.p. verso.
ISBN 0-486-27278-8 (pbk.)
I. Title. II. Series.
PR2807.A1 1992
822.3'3—dc20 92-11424
CIP

Note

WILLIAM SHAKESPEARE (1564–1616) wrote *Hamlet* between 1599 and 1601, creating one of the very greatest and most discussed works in English literature. The playwright did not, however, invent his eponymous hero or the basic features of the plot. Hamlet, the avenging son, was a figure from Danish legend dating back at least as far as the twelfth-century *Historiae Danicae* by Saxo Grammaticus. The Elizabethans were familiar with Saxo through Belleforest's French translation. The immediate source for Shakespeare's play is thought to have been a lost play now known as the *Ur-Hamlet*, possibly written by Thomas Kyd. Influenced by Seneca's tragedies, Kyd was instrumental in securing a place for the revenge drama on the English stage. Although *Hamlet* does incorporate all the stock elements of the revenge tragedy—murder, madness, revenge and supernatural intervention—the play transfigures the form, developing complex characters out of stage types, interweaving philosophical questions with a compelling narrative and offering a brilliant commentary on contemporary stagecraft.

The edition reprinted here is that of the "Cambridge Shakespeare," which combines the texts of the Second Quarto (1604) and the First Folio (1623). Punctuation and orthography have been modernized. The annotations are based on those given in the third edition of Alexander Schmidt's *Shakespeare-Lexicon*.

Contents

Dramatis Personae

CLAUDIUS, King of Denmark.
HAMLET, son to the late, and nephew to the present king.
POLONIUS, Lord Chamberlain.
HORATIO, friend to Hamlet.
LAERTES, son to Polonius.
VOLTIMAND, CORNELIUS, ROSENCRANTZ, GUILDENSTERN, OSRIC, A Gentleman, — courtiers.
A Priest.
MARCELLUS, BERNARDO, — officers.
FRANCISCO, a soldier.
REYNALDO, servant to Polonius.
Players.
Two Clowns, grave-diggers.
FORTINBRAS, Prince of Norway.
A Captain.
English Ambassadors.

GERTRUDE, Queen of Denmark, and mother to Hamlet.
OPHELIA, daughter to Polonius.

Lords, Ladies, Officers, Soldiers, Sailors, Messengers, and other Attendants.

Ghost of Hamlet's Father.

SCENE: *Denmark*.

ACT I.

SCENE I. *Elsinore. A platform before the castle.*

FRANCISCO *at his post. Enter to him* BERNARDO.

BER. Who's there?
FRAN. Nay, answer me. Stand and unfold yourself.
BER. Long live the King!
FRAN. Bernardo?
BER. He.
FRAN. You come most carefully upon your hour.
BER. 'Tis now struck twelve. Get thee to bed, Francisco.
FRAN. For this relief much thanks. 'Tis bitter cold,
And I am sick at heart.
BER. Have you had quiet guard?
FRAN. Not a mouse stirring.
BER. Well, good night.
If you do meet Horatio and Marcellus,
The rivals[1] of my watch, bid them make haste.
FRAN. I think I hear them. Stand, ho! Who is there?

Enter HORATIO *and* MARCELLUS.

HOR. Friends to this ground.
MAR. And liegemen to the Dane.
FRAN. Give you good night.
MAR. O, farewell, honest soldier.
Who hath relieved you?
FRAN. Bernardo hath my place.
Give you good night. [*Exit.*
MAR. Holla, Bernardo!
BER. Say,

[1] *rivals*] partners.

What, is Horatio there?
HOR. A piece of him.
BER. Welcome, Horatio. Welcome, good Marcellus.
MAR. What, has this thing appear'd again tonight?
BER. I have seen nothing.
MAR. Horatio says 'tis but our fantasy,
And will not let belief take hold of him
Touching this dreaded sight, twice seen of us.
Therefore I have entreated him along
With us to watch the minutes of this night,
That if again this apparition come
He may approve our eyes[2] and speak to it.
HOR. Tush, tush, 'twill not appear.
BER. Sit down awhile,
And let us once again assail your ears,
That are so fortified against our story,
What we have two nights seen.
HOR. Well, sit we down,
And let us hear Bernardo speak of this.
BER. Last night of all,
When yond same star that's westward from the pole[3]
Had made his course to illume that part of heaven
Where now it burns, Marcellus and myself,
The bell then beating one—

Enter GHOST.

MAR. Peace, break thee off. Look where it comes again.
BER. In the same figure like the King that's dead.
MAR. Thou art a scholar; speak to it, Horatio.
BER. Looks it not like the King? Mark it, Horatio.
HOR. Most like. It harrows me with fear and wonder.
BER. It would be spoke to.
MAR. Question it, Horatio.
HOR. What art thou that usurp'st this time of night,
Together with that fair and warlike form
In which the majesty of buried Denmark
Did sometimes[4] march? By heaven I charge thee, speak!
MAR. It is offended.
BER. See, it stalks away.

[2] *approve our eyes*] confirm what we have seen.
[3] *pole*] polestar.
[4] *sometimes*] formerly.

HOR. Stay! speak, speak! I charge thee, speak! [*Exit* GHOST.
MAR. 'Tis gone, and will not answer.
BER. How now, Horatio? You tremble and look pale.
Is not this something more than fantasy?
What think you on't?
HOR. Before my God, I might not this believe
Without the sensible and true avouch
Of mine own eyes.
MAR. Is it not like the King?
HOR. As thou art to thyself.
Such was the very armour he had on
When he the ambitious Norway combated;
So frown'd he once, when, in an angry parle,[5]
He smote the sledded Polacks on the ice.
'Tis strange.
MAR. Thus twice before, and jump[6] at this dead hour,
With martial stalk hath he gone by our watch.
HOR. In what particular thought to work I know not;
But, in the gross and scope[7] of my opinion,
This bodes some strange eruption to our state.
MAR. Good now, sit down, and tell me, he that knows,
Why this same strict and most observant watch
So nightly toils the subject of the land,[8]
And why such daily cast[9] of brazen cannon,
And foreign mart[10] for implements of war,
Why such impress[11] of shipwrights, whose sore task
Does not divide the Sunday from the week.
What might be toward, that this sweaty haste
Doth make the night joint-labourer with the day,
Who is't that can inform me?
HOR. That can I—
At least the whisper goes so. Our last King,
Whose image even but now appear'd to us,
Was, as you know, by Fortinbras of Norway,
Thereto prick'd on by a most emulate[12] pride,

[5] *parle*] parley, exchange.
[6] *jump*] exactly.
[7] *gross and scope*] general drift.
[8] *toils . . . land*] causes the people of this land to toil.
[9] *cast*] casting.
[10] *mart*] trading.
[11] *impress*] conscription.
[12] *emulate*] jealous, ambitious.

Dared to the combat; in which our valiant Hamlet—
For so this side of our known world esteem'd him—
Did slay this Fortinbras; who by a seal'd compact,
Well ratified by law and heraldry,
Did forfeit, with his life, all those his lands
Which he stood seized[13] of, to the conqueror;
Against the which, a moiety competent[14]
Was gaged by our King; which had return'd
To the inheritance of Fortinbras,
Had he been vanquisher; as, by the same covenant
And carriage of the article design'd,[15]
His fell to Hamlet. Now, sir, young Fortinbras,
Of unimproved[16] metal hot and full,
Hath in the skirts of Norway here and there
Shark'd up[17] a list of lawless resolutes,[18]
For food and diet to some enterprise
That hath a stomach in't; which is no other—
As it doth well appear unto our state—
But to recover of us, by strong hand
And terms compulsatory, those foresaid lands
So by his father lost. And this, I take it,
Is the main motive of our preparations,
The source of this our watch and the chief head
Of this post-haste and romage[19] in the land.

BER. I think it be no other but e'en so.
Well may it sort[20] that this portentous figure
Comes armed through our watch, so like the King
That was and is the question of these wars.

HOR. A mote it is to trouble the mind's eye.
In the most high and palmy[21] state of Rome,
A little ere the mightiest Julius fell,
The graves stood tenantless, and the sheeted dead
Did squeak and gibber in the Roman streets;
As stars with trains of fire and dews of blood,

[13] *seized*] possessed.
[14] *moiety competent*] sufficient portion.
[15] *carriage . . . design'd*] import of the aforementioned article.
[16] *unimproved*] unemployed, latent.
[17] *Shark'd up*] recruited haphazardly and illegally.
[18] *resolutes*] desperadoes.
[19] *romage*] bustle, activity.
[20] *sort*] be fitting.
[21] *palmy*] glorious.

Disasters[22] in the sun; and the moist star,[23]
Upon whose influence Neptune's empire stands,
Was sick almost to doomsday with eclipse.
And even the like precurse[24] of feared events,
As harbingers preceding still[25] the fates
And prologue to the omen coming on,
Have heaven and earth together demonstrated
Unto our climatures and countrymen.

Enter GHOST.

But soft, behold! Lo, where it comes again.
I'll cross[26] it, though it blast me. Stay, illusion.
If thou hast any sound or use of voice,
Speak to me;
If there be any good thing to be done,
That may to thee do ease and grace to me,
Speak to me;
If thou art privy to thy country's fate,
Which, happily,[27] foreknowing may avoid,
O, speak!
Or if thou hast uphoarded in thy life
Extorted treasure in the womb of earth,
For which, they say, you spirits oft walk in death,
Speak of it; stay and speak. [*The cock crows.*] Stop it, Marcellus.

MAR. Shall I strike at it with my partisan?[28]
HOR. Do, if it will not stand.
BER. 'Tis here.
HOR. 'Tis here.
MAR. 'Tis gone. [*Exit* GHOST.
We do it wrong, being so majestical,
To offer it the show of violence;
For it is, as the air, invulnerable,
And our vain blows malicious mockery.[29]
BER. It was about to speak, when the cock crew.

[22] *Disasters*] ominous signs.
[23] *the moist star*] the moon.
[24] *precurse*] forerunning.
[25] *still*] always.
[26] *cross*] confront.
[27] *happily*] haply, by chance.
[28] *partisan*] long-handled spear.
[29] *malicious mockery*] a mere semblance of malice.

HOR. And then it started like a guilty thing
Upon a fearful summons. I have heard,
The cock, that is the trumpet to the morn,
Doth with his lofty and shrill-sounding throat
Awake the god of day, and at his warning,
Whether in sea or fire, in earth or air,
The extravagant and erring[30] spirit hies
To his confine;[31] and of the truth herein
This present object made probation.[32]

MAR. It faded on the crowing of the cock.
Some say that ever 'gainst[33] that season comes
Wherein our Saviour's birth is celebrated,
The bird of dawning singeth all night long;
And then, they say, no spirit dare stir abroad,
The nights are wholesome, then no planets strike,[34]
No fairy takes[35] nor witch hath power to charm,
So hallow'd and so gracious[36] is the time.

HOR. So have I heard and do in part believe it.
But look, the morn, in russet mantle clad,
Walks o'er the dew of yon high eastward hill.
Break we our watch up; and by my advice,
Let us impart what we have seen tonight
Unto young Hamlet; for, upon my life,
This spirit, dumb to us, will speak to him.
Do you consent we shall acquaint him with it,
As needful in our loves, fitting our duty?

MAR. Let's do't, I pray; and I this morning know
Where we shall find him most conveniently. [*Exeunt.*

[30] *extravagant and erring*] wandering.
[31] *confine*] appointed territory.
[32] *probation*] proof.
[33] *'gainst*] just before.
[34] *strike*] blast, destroy.
[35] *takes*] charms.
[36] *gracious*] blessed.

SCENE II. *A room of state in the castle.*

Flourish. Enter the KING, QUEEN, HAMLET, POLONIUS, LAERTES, VOLTIMAND, CORNELIUS, Lords, *and* Attendants.

KING. Though yet of Hamlet our dear brother's death
The memory be green, and that it us befitted
To bear our hearts in grief and our whole kingdom
To be contracted in one brow of woe,
Yet so far hath discretion fought with nature
That we with wisest sorrow think on him
Together with remembrance of ourselves.
Therefore our sometime sister, now our queen,
The imperial jointress[1] to this warlike state,
Have we, as 'twere with a defeated joy,
With an auspicious and a dropping eye,
With mirth in funeral and with dirge in marriage,
In equal scale weighing delight and dole,
Taken to wife. Nor have we herein barr'd
Your better wisdoms, which have freely gone
With this affair along. For all, our thanks.
Now follows, that you know, young Fortinbras,
Holding a weak supposal[2] of our worth,
Or thinking by our late dear brother's death
Our state to be disjoint and out of frame,
Colleagued with this dream of his advantage,
He hath not fail'd to pester us with message,
Importing the surrender of those lands
Lost by his father, with all bonds of law,
To our most valiant brother. So much for him.
Now for ourself, and for this time of meeting,
Thus much the business is: we have here writ
To Norway, uncle of young Fortinbras—
Who, impotent and bed-rid, scarcely hears
Of this his nephew's purpose—to suppress

[1] *jointress*] dowager.
[2] *weak supposal*] low opinion.

His further gait[3] herein, in that the levies,
The lists and full proportions, are all made
Out of his subject;[4] and we here dispatch
You, good Cornelius, and you, Voltimand,
For bearers of this greeting to old Norway,
Giving to you no further personal power
To business with the King more than the scope
Of these dilated[5] articles allow.
Farewell, and let your haste commend your duty.

COR. }
VOL. } In that and all things will we show our duty.

KING. We doubt it nothing. Heartily farewell.

[*Exeunt* VOLTIMAND *and* CORNELIUS.

And now, Laertes, what's the news with you?
You told us of some suit; what is't, Laertes?
You cannot speak of reason to the Dane,[6]
And lose your voice.[7] What wouldst thou beg, Laertes,
That shall not be my offer, not thy asking?
The head is not more native to the heart,
The hand more instrumental to the mouth,
Than is the throne of Denmark to thy father.
What wouldst thou have, Laertes?

LAER. My dread lord,
Your leave and favour to return to France,
From whence though willingly I came to Denmark,
To show my duty in your coronation,
Yet now, I must confess, that duty done,
My thoughts and wishes bend again toward France
And bow them to your gracious leave and pardon.

KING. Have you your father's leave? What says Polonius?

POL. He hath, my lord, wrung from me my slow leave
By laboursome petition, and at last
Upon his will I seal'd my hard[8] consent.
I do beseech you, give him leave to go.

KING. Take thy fair hour, Laertes; time be thine,
And thy best graces spend it at thy will.

[3] *gait*] proceeding.
[4] *Out of his subject*] at the expense of his people.
[5] *dilated*] detailed, copious.
[6] *the Dane*] the King of Denmark.
[7] *lose your voice*] speak in vain.
[8] *hard*] reluctant.

But now, my cousin[9] Hamlet, and my son—
HAM. [*Aside*] A little more than kin, and less than kind.
KING. How is it that the clouds still hang on you?
HAM. Not so, my lord; I am too much i' the sun.
QUEEN. Good Hamlet, cast thy nighted colour off,
And let thine eye look like a friend on Denmark.
Do not for ever with thy vailed[10] lids
Seek for thy noble father in the dust.
Thou know'st 'tis common: all that lives must die,
Passing through nature to eternity.
HAM. Ay, madam, it is common.
QUEEN. If it be,
Why seems it so particular with thee?
HAM. Seems, madam? Nay, it is. I know not 'seems.'
'Tis not alone my inky cloak, good mother,
Nor customary suits of solemn black,
Nor windy suspiration of forced breath,
No, nor the fruitful river in the eye,
Nor the dejected haviour of the visage,
Together with all forms, moods, shapes of grief,
That can denote me truly. These indeed seem,
For they are actions that a man might play;
But I have that within which passeth show,
These but the trappings and the suits of woe.
KING. 'Tis sweet and commendable in your nature, Hamlet,
To give these mourning duties to your father;
But, you must know, your father lost a father,
That father lost, lost his, and the survivor bound
In filial obligation for some term
To do obsequious sorrow.[11] But to persever
In obstinate condolement is a course
Of impious stubbornness; 'tis unmanly grief;
It shows a will most incorrect[12] to heaven,
A heart unfortified, a mind impatient,
An understanding simple and unschool'd;
For what we know must be and is as common
As any the most vulgar[13] thing to sense,

[9] *cousin*] close relation.
[10] *vailed*] lowered.
[11] *obsequious sorrow*] i.e., mourning appropriate for obsequies.
[12] *incorrect*] recalcitrant.
[13] *vulgar*] ordinary, commonplace.

Why should we in our peevish opposition
Take it to heart? Fie! 'tis a fault to heaven,
A fault against the dead, a fault to nature,
To reason most absurd, whose common theme
Is death of fathers, and who still[14] hath cried,
From the first corse till he that died today,
'This must be so.' We pray you, throw to earth
This unprevailing[15] woe, and think of us
As of a father; for let the world take note,
You are the most immediate[16] to our throne,
And with no less nobility of love
Than that which dearest father bears his son
Do I impart toward you. For your intent
In going back to school in Wittenberg,
It is most retrograde[17] to our desire,
And we beseech you, bend you to remain
Here in the cheer and comfort of our eye,
Our chiefest courtier, cousin and our son.

QUEEN. Let not thy mother lose her prayers, Hamlet.
I pray thee, stay with us; go not to Wittenberg.

HAM. I shall in all my best obey you, madam.

KING. Why, 'tis a loving and a fair reply.
Be as ourself in Denmark. Madam, come;
This gentle and unforced accord of Hamlet
Sits smiling to my heart; in grace whereof,
No jocund health that Denmark drinks today,
But the great cannon to the clouds shall tell,
And the King's rouse[18] the heaven shall bruit[19] again,
Re-speaking earthly thunder. Come away.

[*Flourish. Exeunt all but* HAMLET.

HAM. O, that this too too sullied flesh would melt,
Thaw and resolve itself into a dew,
Or that the Everlasting had not fix'd
His canon 'gainst self-slaughter! O God! God!
How weary, stale, flat and unprofitable
Seem to me all the uses of this world!

[14] *still*] always.
[15] *unprevailing*] unavailing, pointless.
[16] *most immediate*] next in succession.
[17] *retrograde*] contrary.
[18] *rouse*] drink, toast.
[19] *bruit*] announce.

Fie on't! ah fie! 'Tis an unweeded garden
That grows to seed; things rank and gross in nature
Possess it merely.[20] That it should come to this!
But two months dead—nay, not so much, not two—
So excellent a king, that was to this
Hyperion to a satyr, so loving to my mother
That he might not beteem[21] the winds of heaven
Visit her face too roughly. Heaven and earth,
Must I remember? Why, she would hang on him
As if increase of appetite had grown
By what it fed on; and yet, within a month—
Let me not think on't—Frailty, thy name is woman—
A little month, or ere those shoes were old
With which she follow'd my poor father's body,
Like Niobe, all tears—why she, even she—
O God! a beast that wants discourse of reason
Would have mourn'd longer—married with my uncle,
My father's brother, but no more like my father
Than I to Hercules. Within a month,
Ere yet the salt of most unrighteous tears
Had left the flushing in her galled eyes,
She married. O, most wicked speed, to post
With such dexterity to incestuous sheets!
It is not, nor it cannot come to good.
But break, my heart, for I must hold my tongue.

Enter HORATIO, MARCELLUS, *and* BERNARDO.

HOR. Hail to your lordship.
HAM. I am glad to see you well.
Horatio—or I do forget myself.
HOR. The same, my lord, and your poor servant ever.
HAM. Sir, my good friend; I'll change that name[22] with you.
And what make you from Wittenberg, Horatio?—
Marcellus.
MAR. My good lord.
HAM. I am very glad to see you.—[*To* BER.] Good even, sir.—
But what, in faith, make you from Wittenberg?
HOR. A truant disposition, good my lord.
HAM. I would not hear your enemy say so,

[20] *merely*] entirely.
[21] *beteem*] permit.
[22] *change that name*] exchange the name "servant."

Nor shall you do my ear that violence,
To make it truster of your own report
Against yourself. I know you are no truant.
But what is your affair in Elsinore?
We'll teach you to drink deep ere you depart.

HOR. My lord, I came to see your father's funeral.

HAM. I pray thee, do not mock me, fellow-student;
I think it was to see my mother's wedding.

HOR. Indeed, my lord, it follow'd hard upon.

HAM. Thrift, thrift, Horatio. The funeral baked meats
Did coldly furnish forth the marriage tables.
Would I had met my dearest[23] foe in heaven
Or ever[24] I had seen that day, Horatio.
My father—Methinks I see my father.

HOR. O where, my lord?

HAM. In my mind's eye, Horatio.

HOR. I saw him once; he was a goodly king.

HAM. He was a man, take him for all in all;
I shall not look upon his like again.

HOR. My lord, I think I saw him yesternight.

HAM. Saw? Who?

HOR. My lord, the King your father.

HAM. The King my father?

HOR. Season your admiration[25] for a while
With an attent ear, till I may deliver,
Upon the witness of these gentlemen,
This marvel to you.

HAM. For God's love, let me hear!

HOR. Two nights together had these gentlemen,
Marcellus and Bernardo, on their watch,
In the dead vast and middle of the night,
Been thus encounter'd. A figure like your father,
Armed at point exactly,[26] cap-à-pie,[27]
Appears before them, and with solemn march
Goes slow and stately by them. Thrice he walk'd
By their oppress'd and fear-surprised eyes
Within his truncheon's length, whilst they, distill'd

[23] *dearest*] direst.
[24] *Or ever*] before.
[25] *Season your admiration*] temper your astonishment.
[26] *at point exactly*] correctly.
[27] *cap-à-pie*] head to foot.

Almost to jelly with the act[28] of fear,
Stand dumb, and speak not to him. This to me
In dreadful secrecy impart they did;
And I with them the third night kept the watch,
Where, as they had deliver'd, both in time,
Form of the thing, each word made true and good,
The apparition comes. I knew your father;
These hands are not more like.

HAM. But where was this?

MAR. My lord, upon the platform where we watch'd.

HAM. Did you not speak to it?

HOR. My lord, I did,
But answer made it none. Yet once methought
It lifted up it head and did address
Itself to motion, like as it would speak.
But even then the morning cock crew loud,
And at the sound it shrunk in haste away
And vanish'd from our sight.

HAM. 'Tis very strange.

HOR. As I do live, my honour'd lord, 'tis true,
And we did think it writ down in our duty
To let you know of it.

HAM. Indeed, indeed, sirs; but this troubles me.
Hold you the watch tonight?

MAR. } BER. } We do, my lord.

HAM. Arm'd, say you?

MAR. } BER. } Arm'd, my lord.

HAM. From top to toe?

MAR. } BER. } My lord, from head to foot.

HAM. Then saw you not his face?

HOR. O, yes, my lord; he wore his beaver[29] up.

HAM. What look'd he, frowningly?

HOR. A countenance more in sorrow than in anger.

HAM. Pale, or red?

HOR. Nay, very pale.

HAM. And fix'd his eyes upon you?

[28] *act*] effect.
[29] *beaver*] visor (covering lower part of the face).

HOR. Most constantly.
HAM. I would I had been there.
HOR. It would have much amazed you.
HAM. Very like, very like. Stay'd it long?
HOR. While one with moderate haste might tell a hundred.
MAR.
BER. } Longer, longer.
HOR. Not when I saw't.
HAM. His beard was grizzled, no?
HOR. It was as I have seen it in his life,
A sable silver'd.
HAM. I will watch tonight;
Perchance 'twill walk again.
HOR. I warrant it will.
HAM. If it assume my noble father's person,
I'll speak to it, though hell itself should gape
And bid me hold my peace. I pray you all,
If you have hitherto conceal'd this sight,
Let it be tenable in your silence still,
And whatsoever else shall hap tonight,
Give it an understanding, but no tongue.
I will requite your loves. So fare you well.
Upon the platform, 'twixt eleven and twelve,
I'll visit you.
ALL. Our duty to your honour.
HAM. Your loves, as mine to you. Farewell.
[*Exeunt all but* HAMLET.
My father's spirit in arms! All is not well.
I doubt[30] some foul play. Would the night were come.
Till then sit still, my soul. Foul deeds will rise,
Though all the earth o'erwhelm them, to men's eyes. [*Exit.*

[30] *doubt*] suspect.

SCENE III. *A room in Polonius's house.*

Enter LAERTES *and* OPHELIA.

LAER. My necessaries are embark'd. Farewell.
And, sister, as the winds give benefit
And convoy is assistant,[1] do not sleep,
But let me hear from you.
OPH. Do you doubt that?
LAER. For Hamlet, and the trifling of his favour,
Hold it a fashion, and a toy in blood,[2]
A violet in the youth of primy[3] nature,
Forward,[4] not permanent, sweet, not lasting,
The perfume and suppliance[5] of a minute,
No more.
OPH. No more but so?
LAER. Think it no more.
For nature crescent[6] does not grow alone
In thews[7] and bulk, but, as this temple[8] waxes,
The inward service of the mind and soul
Grows wide withal. Perhaps he loves you now,
And now no soil nor cautel[9] doth besmirch
The virtue of his will; but you must fear,
His greatness weigh'd,[10] his will is not his own;
For he himself is subject to his birth.
He may not, as unvalued persons do,
Carve for himself, for on his choice depends
The safety and health of this whole state;
And therefore must his choice be circumscribed

[1] *convoy is assistant*] means of conveyance are available.
[2] *toy in blood*] amorous whim.
[3] *primy*] flourishing.
[4] *Forward*] premature.
[5] *suppliance*] pastime, gratification.
[6] *crescent*] growing.
[7] *thews*] strength.
[8] *temple*] i.e., human body.
[9] *cautel*] deceit.
[10] *His greatness weigh'd*] his important position being considered.

Unto the voice and yielding[11] of that body
Whereof he is the head. Then if he says he loves you,
It fits your wisdom so far to believe it
As he in his particular act and place
May give his saying deed; which is no further
Than the main[12] voice of Denmark goes withal.
Then weigh what loss your honour may sustain
If with too credent ear you list[13] his songs,
Or lose your heart, or your chaste treasure open
To his unmaster'd importunity.
Fear it, Ophelia, fear it, my dear sister,
And keep you in the rear of your affection,
Out of the shot and danger of desire.
The chariest[14] maid is prodigal enough
If she unmask her beauty to the moon.
Virtue itself 'scapes not calumnious strokes.
The canker galls the infants of the spring
Too oft before their buttons[15] be disclosed,
And in the morn and liquid[16] dew of youth
Contagious blastments[17] are most imminent.
Be wary then; best safety lies in fear.
Youth to itself rebels, though none else near.

OPH. I shall the effect of this good lesson keep
As watchman to my heart. But, good my brother,
Do not, as some ungracious[18] pastors do,
Show me the steep and thorny way to heaven,
Whilst, like a puff'd and reckless libertine,
Himself the primrose path of dalliance treads
And recks not his own rede.[19]

LAER. O, fear me not.
I stay too long. But here my father comes.

Enter POLONIUS.

A double blessing is a double grace;

[11] *yielding*] consent.
[12] *main*] general.
[13] *list*] listen to.
[14] *chariest*] most modest.
[15] *buttons*] buds.
[16] *liquid*] pure, limpid.
[17] *blastments*] blights.
[18] *ungracious*] impious.
[19] *recks not his own rede*] does not heed his own advice.

Occasion smiles upon a second leave.
POL. Yet here, Laertes? Aboard, aboard, for shame!
The wind sits in the shoulder of your sail,
And you are stay'd for. There, my blessing with thee.
And these few precepts in thy memory
Look thou character.[20] Give thy thoughts no tongue,
Nor any unproportion'd thought his act.
Be thou familiar, but by no means vulgar.
Those friends thou hast, and their adoption tried,[21]
Grapple them to thy soul with hoops of steel,
But do not dull thy palm with entertainment
Of each new-hatch'd unfledged comrade. Beware
Of entrance to a quarrel; but being in,
Bear't, that the opposed may beware of thee.
Give every man thy ear, but few thy voice;
Take each man's censure,[22] but reserve thy judgement.
Costly thy habit[23] as thy purse can buy,
But not express'd in fancy; rich, not gaudy;
For the apparel oft proclaims the man;
And they in France of the best rank and station
Are of a most select and generous chief[24] in that.
Neither a borrower nor a lender be;
For loan oft loses both itself and friend,
And borrowing dulls the edge of husbandry.[25]
This above all: to thine own self be true,
And it must follow, as the night the day,
Thou canst not then be false to any man.
Farewell. My blessing season this in thee.
LAER. Most humbly do I take my leave, my lord.
POL. The time invites you; go, your servants tend.
LAER. Farewell, Ophelia, and remember well
What I have said to you.
OPH. 'Tis in my memory lock'd,
And you yourself shall keep the key of it.
LAER. Farewell. [*Exit.*
POL. What is't, Ophelia, he hath said to you?

[20] *character*] inscribe.
[21] *tried*] justified.
[22] *censure*] opinion.
[23] *habit*] dress.
[24] *chief*] excellence.
[25] *husbandry*] economy, saving.

OPH. So please you, something touching the Lord Hamlet.
POL. Marry, well bethought.
'Tis told me, he hath very oft of late
Given private time to you, and you yourself
Have of your audience been most free and bounteous.
If it be so—as so 'tis put on[26] me,
And that in way of caution—I must tell you,
You do not understand yourself so clearly
As it behoves my daughter and your honour.
What is between you? Give me up the truth.
OPH. He hath, my lord, of late made many tenders
Of his affection to me.
POL. Affection? Pooh! You speak like a green girl,
Unsifted[27] in such perilous circumstance.
Do you believe his tenders, as you call them?
OPH. I do not know, my lord, what I should think.
POL. Marry, I'll teach you. Think yourself a baby,
That you have ta'en these tenders for true pay,
Which are not sterling.[28] Tender yourself more dearly;[29]
Or—not to crack the wind of the poor phrase,
Running it thus—you'll tender me a fool.
OPH. My lord, he hath importuned me with love
In honourable fashion.
POL. Ay, fashion you may call it. Go to, go to.
OPH. And hath given countenance[30] to his speech, my lord,
With almost all the holy vows of heaven.
POL. Ay, springes[31] to catch woodcocks. I do know,
When the blood burns, how prodigal the soul
Lends the tongue vows. These blazes, daughter,
Giving more light than heat, extinct in both,
Even in their promise, as it is a-making,
You must not take for fire. From this time
Be something scanter of your maiden presence;
Set your entreatments[32] at a higher rate

[26] *put on*] impressed upon.
[27] *unsifted*] inexperienced.
[28] *sterling*] of genuine value. Polonius is playing on two meanings of "tender": (1) to proffer affection; (2) to pay money.
[29] *Tender . . . dearly*] (1) Take care of yourself; (2) set a higher price on yourself.
[30] *countenance*] authority.
[31] *springes*] snares.
[32] *entreatments*] exchanges.

Than a command to parley.[33] For Lord Hamlet,
Believe so much in him, that he is young,
And with a larger tether may he walk
Than may be given you. In few,[34] Ophelia,
Do not believe his vows; for they are brokers,[35]
Not of that dye which their investments[36] show,
But mere implorators[37] of unholy suits,
Breathing[38] like sanctified and pious bawds,
The better to beguile. This is for all:
I would not, in plain terms, from this time forth,
Have you so slander any moment leisure,
As to give words or talk with the Lord Hamlet.
Look to't, I charge you. Come your ways.

OPH. I shall obey, my lord. [*Exeunt.*

SCENE IV. *The platform.*

Enter HAMLET, HORATIO, *and* MARCELLUS.

HAM. The air bites shrewdly;[1] it is very cold.

HOR. It is a nipping and an eager[2] air.

HAM. What hour now?

HOR. I think it lacks of twelve.

MAR. No, it is struck.

HOR. Indeed? I heard it not. It then draws near the season
Wherein the spirit held his wont to walk.
[*A flourish of trumpets, and ordnance shot off within.*
What doth this mean, my lord?

HAM. The King doth wake tonight and takes his rouse,[3]

[33] *command to parley*] invitation to talk.
[34] *In few*] in short.
[35] *brokers*] go-betweens, panders.
[36] *investments*] clothes.
[37] *implorators*] implorers.
[38] *Breathing*] speaking.

---

[1] *shrewdly*] keenly.
[2] *eager*] biting, bitter.
[3] *takes his rouse*] carouses.

Keeps wassail,[4] and the swaggering upspring[5] reels;
And as he drains his draughts of Rhenish down,
The kettle-drum and trumpet thus bray out
The triumph[6] of his pledge.

HOR. Is it a custom?

HAM. Ay, marry, is't;
But to my mind, though I am native here
And to the manner born, it is a custom
More honour'd in the breach than the observance.
This heavy-headed revel east and west
Makes us traduced and tax'd of[7] other nations.
They clepe[8] us drunkards, and with swinish phrase
Soil our addition;[9] and indeed it takes
From our achievements, though perform'd at height,
The pith and marrow of our attribute.[10]
So, oft it chances in particular men,[11]
That for some vicious mole of nature in them,
As in their birth—wherein they are not guilty,
Since nature cannot choose his origin—
By the o'ergrowth of some complexion,[12]
Oft breaking down the pales[13] and forts of reason,
Or by some habit that too much o'er-leavens[14]
The form of plausive[15] manners, that these men—
Carrying, I say, the stamp of one defect,
Being Nature's livery, or Fortune's star—
Their virtues else—be they as pure as grace,
As infinite as man may undergo—[16]
Shall in the general censure take corruption
From that particular fault. The dram of evil
Doth all the noble substance of a doubt[17]

[4] *keeps wassail*] carouses.
[5] *upspring*] wild German dance.
[6] *triumph*] celebration.
[7] *tax'd of*] censured by.
[8] *clepe*] call.
[9] *with swinish . . . addition*] by calling us swine sully our reputation.
[10] *attribute*] reputation.
[11] *particular men*] individuals.
[12] *complexion*] humor, trait.
[13] *pales*] palings.
[14] *o'er-leavens*] corrupts.
[15] *plausive*] pleasing.
[16] *undergo*] sustain.
[17] *of a doubt*] the text seems to be corrupt here.

To his own scandal.

Enter GHOST.

HOR. Look, my lord, it comes.
HAM. Angels and ministers of grace defend us!
Be thou a spirit of health or goblin damn'd,
Bring with thee airs from heaven or blasts from hell,
Be thy intents wicked or charitable,
Thou comest in such a questionable[18] shape
That I will speak to thee. I'll call thee Hamlet,
King, father, royal Dane. O, answer me!
Let me not burst in ignorance, but tell
Why thy canonized bones, hearsed[19] in death,
Have burst their cerements, why the sepulchre,
Wherein we saw thee quietly inurn'd,
Hath oped his ponderous and marble jaws,
To cast thee up again. What may this mean,
That thou, dead corse, again, in complete steel,
Revisits thus the glimpses of the moon,
Making night hideous, and we fools of nature[20]
So horridly to shake our disposition
With thoughts beyond the reaches of our souls?
Say, why is this? Wherefore? What should we do?
[GHOST *beckons* HAMLET.
HOR. It beckons you to go away with it,
As if it some impartment[21] did desire
To you alone.
MAR. Look, with what courteous action
It waves you to a more removed ground.
But do not go with it.
HOR. No, by no means.
HAM. It will not speak. Then I will follow it.
HOR. Do not, my lord.
HAM. Why, what should be the fear?
I do not set my life at a pin's fee;
And for my soul, what can it do to that,
Being a thing immortal as itself?
It waves me forth again. I'll follow it.

[18] *questionable*] inviting question.
[19] *hearsed*] coffined.
[20] *fools of nature*] beings limited to the understanding of things natural.
[21] *impartment*] communication.

HOR. What if it tempt you toward the flood, my lord,
Or to the dreadful summit of the cliff
That beetles o'er[22] his base into the sea,
And there assume some other horrible form,
Which might deprive your sovereignty of reason
And draw you into madness? Think of it.
The very place puts toys of desperation,[23]
Without more motive, into every brain
That looks so many fathoms to the sea
And hears it roar beneath.

HAM. It waves me still.
Go on; I'll follow thee.

MAR. You shall not go, my lord.

HAM. Hold off your hands.

HOR. Be ruled; you shall not go.

HAM. My fate cries out,
And makes each petty artery in this body
As hardy as the Nemean lion's[24] nerve.
Still am I call'd. Unhand me, gentlemen.
By heaven, I'll make a ghost of him that lets[25] me.
I say, away! Go on; I'll follow thee.
[*Exeunt* GHOST *and* HAMLET.

HOR. He waxes desperate with imagination.

MAR. Let's follow. 'Tis not fit thus to obey him.

HOR. Have after. To what issue will this come?

MAR. Something is rotten in the state of Denmark.

HOR. Heaven will direct it.

MAR. Nay, let's follow him. [*Exeunt.*

[22] *beetles o'er*] overhangs.
[23] *toys of desperation*] freakish thoughts of suicide.
[24] *Nemean lion's*] The Nemean lion was slain by Hercules as the first of his twelve labors.
[25] *lets*] hinders.

SCENE V. *Another part of the platform.*

Enter GHOST *and* HAMLET.

HAM. Whither wilt thou lead me? Speak; I'll go no further.
GHOST. Mark me.
HAM. I will.
GHOST. My hour is almost come,
When I to sulphurous and tormenting flames
Must render up myself.
HAM. Alas, poor ghost!
GHOST. Pity me not, but lend thy serious hearing
To what I shall unfold.
HAM. Speak; I am bound to hear.
GHOST. So art thou to revenge, when thou shalt hear.
HAM. What?
GHOST. I am thy father's spirit,
Doom'd for a certain term to walk the night,
And for the day confined to fast in fires,
Till the foul crimes done in my days of nature
Are burnt and purged away. But that I am forbid
To tell the secrets of my prison-house,
I could a tale unfold whose lightest word
Would harrow up thy soul, freeze thy young blood,
Make thy two eyes, like stars, start from their spheres,
Thy knotted and combined locks to part
And each particular hair to stand an end,
Like quills upon the fretful porpentine.
But this eternal blazon[1] must not be
To ears of flesh and blood. List, list, O, list!
If thou didst ever thy dear father love—
HAM. O God!
GHOST. Revenge his foul and most unnatural murder.
HAM. Murder?
GHOST. Murder most foul, as in the best it is,
But this most foul, strange, and unnatural.
HAM. Haste me to know't, that I, with wings as swift

[1] *eternal blazon*] description of the afterlife.

As meditation or the thoughts of love,
May sweep to my revenge.
GHOST. I find thee apt;
And duller shouldst thou be than the fat weed
That roots itself in ease on Lethe[2] wharf,
Wouldst thou not stir in this. Now, Hamlet, hear.
'Tis given out that, sleeping in my orchard,[3]
A serpent stung me; so the whole ear of Denmark
Is by a forged process[4] of my death
Rankly abused. But know, thou noble youth,
The serpent that did sting thy father's life
Now wears his crown.
HAM. O my prophetic soul! My uncle!
GHOST. Ay, that incestuous, that adulterate beast,
With witchcraft of his wit, with traitorous gifts—
O wicked wit and gifts that have the power
So to seduce!—won to his shameful lust
The will of my most seeming-virtuous queen.
O Hamlet, what a falling off was there!
From me, whose love was of that dignity
That it went hand in hand even with the vow
I made to her in marriage; and to decline
Upon a wretch, whose natural gifts were poor
To those of mine.
But virtue, as it never will be moved,
Though lewdness court it in a shape of heaven,
So lust, though to a radiant angel link'd,
Will sate itself in a celestial bed
And prey on garbage.
But, soft! methinks I scent the morning air;
Brief let me be. Sleeping within my orchard,
My custom always of the afternoon,
Upon my secure[5] hour thy uncle stole,
With juice of cursed hebenon in a vial,
And in the porches of my ears did pour
The leperous distilment, whose effect
Holds such an enmity with blood of man
That swift as quicksilver it courses through

[2] *Lethe*] the river of forgetfulness in the underworld.
[3] *orchard*] garden.
[4] *process*] account.
[5] *secure*] free from apprehension, unsuspecting.

The natural gates and alleys of the body,
And with a sudden vigour it doth posset[6]
And curd, like eager[7] droppings into milk,
The thin and wholesome blood. So did it mine;
And a most instant tetter[8] bark'd about,
Most lazar-like,[9] with vile and loathsome crust,
All my smooth body.
Thus was I, sleeping, by a brother's hand
Of life, of crown, of queen, at once dispatch'd,[10]
Cut off even in the blossoms of my sin,
Unhousel'd, disappointed, unaneled,[11]
No reckoning made, but sent to my account
With all my imperfections on my head.
O, horrible! O, horrible! most horrible!
If thou hast nature in thee, bear it not.
Let not the royal bed of Denmark be
A couch for luxury[12] and damned incest.
But, howsoever thou pursuest this act,
Taint not thy mind, nor let thy soul contrive
Against thy mother aught. Leave her to heaven,
And to those thorns that in her bosom lodge,
To prick and sting her. Fare thee well at once.
The glow-worm shows the matin[13] to be near,
And 'gins to pale his uneffectual fire.
Adieu, adieu, adieu. Remember me. [*Exit.*

HAM. O all you host of heaven! O earth! What else?
And shall I couple[14] hell? O, fie! Hold, hold, my heart;
And you, my sinews, grow not instant old,
But bear me stiffly up. Remember thee?
Ay, thou poor ghost, while memory holds a seat
In this distracted globe.[15] Remember thee?
Yea, from the table[16] of my memory

[6] *posset*] curdle, in the manner of a posset (a hot drink of spiced milk mixed with wine or ale).
[7] *eager*] sour.
[8] *tetter*] skin disease.
[9] *lazar-like*] like a leper.
[10] *dispatch'd*] deprived.
[11] *Unhousel'd, disappointed, unaneled*] not having received the sacrament, unprepared and not having received extreme unction.
[12] *luxury*] lechery.
[13] *matin*] morning.
[14] *couple*] include.
[15] *globe*] head.
[16] *table*] (writing) tablet.

I'll wipe away all trivial fond[17] records,
All saws[18] of books, all forms, all pressures[19] past,
That youth and observation copied there;
And thy commandment all alone shall live
Within the book and volume of my brain,
Unmix'd with baser matter. Yes, by heaven!
O most pernicious woman!
O villain, villain, smiling, damned villain!
My tables[20]—meet it is I set it down
That one may smile, and smile, and be a villain;
At least I'm sure it may be so in Denmark. [*Writing*.
So, uncle, there you are. Now to my word.[21]
It is 'Adieu, adieu, remember me.'
I have sworn't.

HOR.
MAR. } [*Within*] My lord, my lord.

Enter HORATIO *and* MARCELLUS.

MAR. Lord Hamlet.
HOR. Heaven secure[22] him!
HAM. So be it.
MAR. Illo, ho, ho, my lord.
HAM. Hillo, ho, ho, boy. Come, bird, come.
MAR. How is't, my noble lord?
HOR. What news, my lord?
HAM. O, wonderful!
HOR. Good my lord, tell it.
HAM. No; you will reveal it.
HOR. Not I, my lord, by heaven.
MAR. Nor I, my lord.
HAM. How say you, then; would heart of man once think it?
But you'll be secret?
HOR.
MAR. } Ay, by heaven, my lord.
HAM. There's ne'er a villain dwelling in all Denmark
But he's an arrant knave.
HOR. There needs no ghost, my lord, come from the grave

17 *fond*] foolish.
18 *saws*] maxims.
19 *pressures*] impressions.
20 *tables*] portable writing-tablets.
21 *word*] watchword, motto.
22 *secure*] protect.

To tell us this.

HAM. Why, right, you are i' the right;
And so, without more circumstance at all,
I hold it fit that we shake hands and part,
You, as your business and desire shall point you—
For every man hath business and desire,
Such as it is—and for my own poor part,
Look you, I'll go pray.

HOR. These are but wild and whirling words, my lord.

HAM. I'm sorry they offend you, heartily;
Yes, faith, heartily.

HOR. There's no offence, my lord.

HAM. Yes, by Saint Patrick,[23] but there is, Horatio,
And much offence too. Touching this vision here,
It is an honest[24] ghost, that let me tell you.
For your desire to know what is between us,
O'ermaster't as you may. And now, good friends,
As you are friends, scholars and soldiers,
Give me one poor request.

HOR. What is't, my lord? We will.

HAM. Never make known what you have seen tonight.

HOR., MAR. My lord, we will not.

HAM. Nay, but swear't.

HOR. In faith,
My lord, not I.

MAR. Nor I, my lord, in faith.

HAM. Upon my sword.[25]

MAR. We have sworn, my lord, already.

HAM. Indeed, upon my sword, indeed.

GHOST. [*Beneath*] Swear.

HAM. Ah, ha, boy, say'st thou so? Art thou there, truepenny?[26]
Come on. You hear this fellow in the cellarage.
Consent to swear.

HOR. Propose the oath, my lord.

HAM. Never to speak of this that you have seen,
Swear by my sword.

GHOST. [*Beneath*] Swear.

[23] *Saint Patrick*] The Irish saint was said to be the keeper of Purgatory.
[24] *honest*] real.
[25] *sword*] The sword's hilt forms a cross.
[26] *truepenny*] honest fellow.

HAM. *Hic et ubique?*[27] Then we'll shift our ground.
Come hither, gentlemen,
And lay your hands again upon my sword.
Never to speak of this that you have heard,
Swear by my sword.

GHOST. [*Beneath*] Swear.

HAM. Well said, old mole. Canst work i' the earth so fast?
A worthy pioner![28] Once more remove, good friends.

HOR. O day and night, but this is wondrous strange.

HAM. And therefore as a stranger give it welcome.
There are more things in heaven and earth, Horatio,
Than are dreamt of in your philosophy.
But come;
Here, as before, never, so help you mercy,
How strange or odd soe'er I bear myself—
As I perchance hereafter shall think meet
To put an antic[29] disposition on—
That you, at such times seeing me, never shall,
With arms encumber'd[30] thus, or this head-shake,
Or by pronouncing of some doubtful phrase,
As 'Well, we know,' or 'We could, an if we would,'
Or 'If we list to speak,' or 'There be, an if they might,'
Or such ambiguous giving out,[31] to note[32]
That you know aught of me; this not to do,
So grace and mercy at your most need help you,
Swear.

GHOST. [*Beneath*] Swear.

HAM. Rest, rest, perturbed spirit. [*They swear.*] So, gentlemen,
With all my love I do commend me to you;
And what so poor a man as Hamlet is
May do to express his love and friending to you,
God willing, shall not lack. Let us go in together;
And still[33] your fingers on your lips, I pray.
The time is out of joint. O cursed spite,
That ever I was born to set it right!
Nay, come, let's go together. [*Exeunt.*

[27] *Hic et ubique*] here and everywhere.
[28] *pioner*] miner, digger.
[29] *antic*] odd, strange.
[30] *encumber'd*] folded.
[31] *giving out*] intimation.
[32] *note*] show.
[33] *still*] always.

ACT II.

SCENE I. *A room in Polonius's house.*

Enter POLONIUS *and* REYNALDO.

POL. Give him this money and these notes, Reynaldo.
REY. I will, my lord.
POL. You shall do marvellous wisely, good Reynaldo,
Before you visit him, to make inquire
Of his behaviour.
REY. My lord, I did intend it.
POL. Marry, well said, very well said. Look you, sir,
Inquire me first what Danskers[1] are in Paris,
And how, and who, what means, and where they keep,[2]
What company, at what expense, and finding
By this encompassment[3] and drift of question
That they do know my son, come you more nearer
Than your particular demands will touch it.[4]
Take[5] you, as 'twere, some distant knowledge of him,
As thus, 'I know his father and his friends,
And in part him.' Do you mark this, Reynaldo?
REY. Ay, very well, my lord.
POL. 'And in part him; but,' you may say, 'not well;
But if't be he I mean, he's very wild,
Addicted so and so;' and there put on him
What forgeries you please—marry, none so rank
As may dishonour him, take heed of that—
But, sir, such wanton, wild and usual slips

[1] *Danskers*] Danes.
[2] *keep*] dwell.
[3] *encompassment*] roundabout way of talking.
[4] *come . . . it*] you will find out more than by asking direct questions.
[5] *Take*] assume.

As are companions noted and most known
To youth and liberty.
REY. As gaming, my lord?
POL. Ay, or drinking, fencing, swearing, quarrelling,
Drabbing.[6] You may go so far.
REY. My lord, that would dishonour him.
POL. 'Faith, no; as you may season it in the charge.
You must not put another scandal on him,
That he is open to incontinency.[7]
That's not my meaning; but breathe his faults so quaintly[8]
That they may seem the taints of liberty,
The flash and outbreak of a fiery mind,
A savageness in unreclaimed[9] blood,
Of general assault.[10]
REY. But, my good lord—
POL. Wherefore should you do this?
REY. Ay, my lord,
I would know that.
POL. Marry, sir, here's my drift,
And I believe it is a fetch of warrant:[11]
You laying these slight sullies on my son,
As 'twere a thing a little soil'd i' the working,
Mark you,
Your party in converse,[12] him you would sound,
Having ever seen in the prenominate[13] crimes
The youth you breathe of guilty, be assured
He closes[14] with you in this consequence:
'Good sir,' or so, or 'friend,' or 'gentleman,'
According to the phrase or the addition[15]
Of man and country.
REY. Very good, my lord.
POL. And then, sir, does he this—he does—what was I about to say?
By the mass, I was about to say something. Where did I leave?

[6] *Drabbing*] whoring.
[7] *incontinency*] habitual licentiousness.
[8] *quaintly*] skillfully, delicately.
[9] *unreclaimed*] untamed.
[10] *Of general assault*] to which all young men are liable.
[11] *fetch of warrant*] justified strategem.
[12] *converse*] conversation.
[13] *prenominate*] aforementioned.
[14] *closes*] agrees.
[15] *addition*] title.

REY. At 'closes in the consequence,' at 'friend or so,' and 'gentleman.'

POL. At 'closes in the consequence,' ay, marry.
He closes with you thus: 'I know the gentleman;
I saw him yesterday,' or 't'other day,'
Or then, or then, with such, or such, 'and, as you say,
There was a[16] gaming,' 'there o'ertook in's rouse,'[17]
'There falling out at tennis;' or perchance,
'I saw him enter such a house of sale,'
Videlicet,[18] a brothel, or so forth.
See you now;
Your bait of falsehood takes this carp of truth;
And thus do we of wisdom and of reach,[19]
With windlasses[20] and with assays of bias,[21]
By indirections find directions out.
So, by my former lecture and advice,
Shall you my son. You have me, have you not?

REY. My lord, I have.

POL. God be wi' ye. Fare ye well.

REY. Good my lord.

POL. Observe his inclination in yourself.[22]

REY. I shall, my lord.

POL. And let him ply his music.

REY. Well, my lord.

POL. Farewell. [*Exit* REYNALDO.

Enter OPHELIA.

How now, Ophelia, what's the matter?

OPH. O, my lord, my lord, I have been so affrighted.

POL. With what, i' the name of God?

OPH. My lord, as I was sewing in my closet,
Lord Hamlet, with his doublet all unbraced,[23]
No hat upon his head, his stockings foul'd,
Ungarter'd and down-gyved[24] to his ankle,

[16] *a*] he.
[17] *o'ertook in's rouse*] overcome by drinking.
[18] *Videlicet*] namely.
[19] *reach*] ability.
[20] *windlasses*] indirect advances.
[21] *assays of bias*] courses that resemble the curved path of a bowling ball.
[22] *Observe . . . yourself*](?) Behave as he does.
[23] *unbraced*] unbuttoned.
[24] *down-gyved*] fallen down and thereby resembling gyves (fetters).

Pale as his shirt, his knees knocking each other,
And with a look so piteous in purport
As if he had been loosed out of hell
To speak of horrors, he comes before me.

POL. Mad for thy love?

OPH. My lord, I do not know,
But truly I do fear it.

POL. What said he?

OPH. He took me by the wrist and held me hard;
Then goes he to the length of all his arm,[25]
And with his other hand thus o'er his brow,
He falls to such perusal of my face
As he would draw it. Long stay'd he so.
At last, a little shaking of mine arm,
And thrice his head thus waving up and down,
He raised a sigh so piteous and profound
As it did seem to shatter all his bulk[26]
And end his being. That done, he lets me go,
And with his head over his shoulder turn'd,
He seem'd to find his way without his eyes;
For out o' doors he went without their helps,
And to the last bended their light on me.

POL. Come, go with me. I will go seek the King.
This is the very ecstasy[27] of love,
Whose violent property fordoes itself[28]
And leads the will to desperate undertakings
As oft as any passion under heaven
That does afflict our natures. I am sorry.
What, have you given him any hard words of late?

OPH. No, my good lord, but, as you did command,
I did repel his letters and denied
His access to me.

POL. That hath made him mad.
I am sorry that with better heed and judgement
I had not quoted[29] him. I fear'd he did but trifle
And meant to wrack thee. But beshrew my jealousy![30]

[25] *goes . . . arm*] withdraws to arm's length.
[26] *bulk*] body, in particular the trunk.
[27] *ecstasy*] madness.
[28] *Whose . . . itself*] the violent nature of which destroys itself.
[29] *quoted*] observed.
[30] *jealousy*] suspicion.

By heaven, it is as proper to our age
To cast beyond ourselves in our opinions
As it is common for the younger sort
To lack discretion. Come, go we to the King.
This must be known, which, being kept close, might move
More grief to hide than hate to utter love.[31]
Come. [*Exeunt.*

SCENE II. *A room in the castle.*

Flourish. Enter KING, QUEEN, ROSENCRANTZ, GUILDENSTERN, *and* Attendants.

KING. Welcome, dear Rosencrantz and Guildenstern.
Moreover[1] that we much did long to see you,
The need we have to use you did provoke
Our hasty sending. Something have you heard
Of Hamlet's transformation—so call it,
Sith[2] nor the exterior nor the inward man
Resembles that it was. What it should be,
More than his father's death, that thus hath put him
So much from the understanding of himself,
I cannot dream of. I entreat you both
That, being of so young days brought up with him
And sith so neighbour'd to his youth and haviour,
That you vouchsafe your rest[3] here in our court
Some little time: so by your companies
To draw him on to pleasures, and to gather
So much as from occasion[4] you may glean,
Whether aught to us unknown afflicts him thus
That open'd lies within our remedy.

QUEEN. Good gentlemen, he hath much talk'd of you,

[31] *might move . . . love*] might cause more grief by being concealed than hatred by being exposed as love.

---

[1] *Moreover*] besides the fact.
[2] *Sith*] since.
[3] *vouchsafe your rest*] agree to stay.
[4] *occasion*] opportunity.

And sure I am two men there are not living
To whom he more adheres. If it will please you
To show us so much gentry[5] and good will
As to expend your time with us awhile
For the supply and profit[6] of our hope,
Your visitation shall receive such thanks
As fits a king's remembrance.

ROS. Both your Majesties
Might, by the sovereign power you have of us,
Put your dread pleasures more into command
Than to entreaty.

GUIL. But we both obey,
And here give up ourselves, in the full bent[7]
To lay our service freely at your feet,
To be commanded.

KING. Thanks, Rosencrantz and gentle Guildenstern.

QUEEN. Thanks, Guildenstern and gentle Rosencrantz.
And I beseech you instantly to visit
My too much changed son. Go, some of you,
And bring these gentlemen where Hamlet is.

GUIL. Heavens make our presence and our practices
Pleasant and helpful to him.

QUEEN. Ay, amen.

[*Exeunt* ROSENCRANTZ, GUILDENSTERN, *and some* Attendants.

Enter POLONIUS.

POL. The ambassadors from Norway, my good lord,
Are joyfully return'd.

KING. Thou still[8] hast been the father of good news.

POL. Have I, my lord? I assure my good liege,
I hold my duty as I hold my soul,
Both to my God and to my gracious King.
And I do think, or else this brain of mine
Hunts not the trail of policy so sure
As it hath used to do, that I have found
The very cause of Hamlet's lunacy.

KING. O, speak of that; that do I long to hear.

POL. Give first admittance to the ambassadors.

[5] *gentry*] courtesy.
[6] *supply and profit*] support and fulfillment.
[7] *in the full bent*] to the utmost extent.
[8] *still*] always.

My news shall be the fruit to that great feast.

KING. Thyself do grace to them, and bring them in.

[*Exit* POLONIUS.

He tells me, my dear Gertrude, he hath found
The head and source of all your son's distemper.

QUEEN. I doubt[9] it is no other but the main:
His father's death and our o'erhasty marriage.

KING. Well, we shall sift him.[10]

Enter POLONIUS, *with* VOLTIMAND *and* CORNELIUS.

Welcome, my good friends.
Say, Voltimand, what from our brother Norway?

VOLT. Most fair return of greetings and desires.
Upon our first,[11] he sent out to suppress
His nephew's levies, which to him appear'd
To be a preparation 'gainst the Polack,[12]
But better look'd into, he truly found
It was against your Highness; whereat grieved,
That so his sickness, age and impotence
Was falsely borne in hand,[13] sends out arrests
On Fortinbras; which he, in brief, obeys,
Receives rebuke from Norway, and in fine[14]
Makes vow before his uncle never more
To give the assay of arms[15] against your Majesty.
Whereon old Norway, overcome with joy,
Gives him three thousand crowns in annual fee
And his commission to employ those soldiers,
So levied as before, against the Polack,
With an entreaty, herein further shown, [*Giving a paper.*
That it might please you to give quiet pass
Through your dominions for this enterprise,
On such regards of safety and allowance[16]

[9] *doubt*] suspect.

[10] *sift him*] question him (Polonius).

[11] *our first*] i.e., our first mentioning the actions of Fortinbras.

[12] *the Polack*] the King of Poland.

[13] *borne in hand*] abused, deluded.

[14] *in fine*] in the end.

[15] *assay of arms*] attack.

[16] *safety and allowance*] safety of Denmark and permission for the Norwegian troops to pass through.

As therein are set down.

KING. It likes us well,
And at our more consider'd time[17] we'll read,
Answer, and think upon this business.
Meantime we thank you for your well-took labour.
Go to your rest; at night we'll feast together.
Most welcome home. [*Exeunt* VOLTIMAND *and* CORNELIUS.

POL. This business is well ended.
My liege, and madam, to expostulate
What majesty should be, what duty is,
Why day is day, night night, and time is time,
Were nothing but to waste night, day and time.
Therefore, since brevity is the soul of wit
And tediousness the limbs and outward flourishes,
I will be brief. Your noble son is mad.
Mad call I it; for, to define true madness,
What is't but to be nothing else but mad?
But let that go.

QUEEN. More matter, with less art.

POL. Madam, I swear I use no art at all.
That he is mad, 'tis true; 'tis true 'tis pity;
And pity 'tis 'tis true—a foolish figure;
But farewell it, for I will use no art.
Mad let us grant him then. And now remains
That we find out the cause of this effect,
Or rather say, the cause of this defect,
For this effect defective comes by cause.
Thus it remains and the remainder thus:
Perpend;[18]
I have a daughter—have while she is mine—
Who in her duty and obedience, mark,
Hath given me this. Now gather and surmise. [*Reads.*

To the celestial, and my soul's idol, the most beautified Ophelia—

That's an ill phrase, a vile phrase; 'beautified' is a vile phrase.
But you shall hear: [*Reads.*

In her excellent white bosom, these, &c.

QUEEN. Came this from Hamlet to her?

POL. Good madam, stay awhile. I will be faithful. [*Reads.*

[17] *more consider'd time*] convenience.
[18] *Perpend*] consider.

Doubt thou the stars are fire,
Doubt that the sun doth move,
Doubt[19] truth to be a liar,
But never doubt I love.

O dear Ophelia, I am ill at these numbers.[20] I have not art to reckon[21] my groans. But that I love thee best, O most best, believe it. Adieu.
Thine evermore, most dear lady, whilst this
machine[22] is to him, HAMLET.

This in obedience hath my daughter shown me;
And more above, hath his solicitings,
As they fell out by time, by means and place,
All given to mine ear.

KING. But how hath she
Received his love?

POL. What do you think of me?

KING. As of a man faithful and honourable.

POL. I would fain prove so. But what might you think,
When I had seen this hot love on the wing—
As I perceived it, I must tell you that,
Before my daughter told me—what might you,
Or my dear Majesty your queen here, think,
If I had play'd the desk or table-book,[23]
Or given my heart a winking,[24] mute and dumb,
Or look'd upon this love with idle sight;[25]
What might you think? No, I went round[26] to work,
And my young mistress thus I did bespeak:
'Lord Hamlet is a prince, out of thy star.
This must not be.' And then I prescripts gave her,
That she should lock herself from his resort,
Admit no messengers, receive no tokens.
Which done, she took the fruits of my advice;
And he, repulsed—a short tale to make—
Fell into a sadness, then into a fast,
Thence to a watch,[27] thence into a weakness,

[19] *Doubt*] suspect.
[20] *ill at these numbers*] not gifted in versifying.
[21] *reckon*] (1) count; (2) put into verse.
[22] *machine*] body.
[23] *play'd . . . table-book*] served as a go-between.
[24] *given . . . winking*] shut my eyes deliberately.
[25] *idle sight*] thoughtlessly.
[26] *round*] straight.
[27] *a watch*] insomnia.

Thence to a lightness,[28] and by this declension[29]
Into the madness wherein now he raves
And all we mourn for.

KING. Do you think 'tis this?

QUEEN. It may be; very like.

POL. Hath there been such a time—I'ld fain know that—
That I have positively said ' 'Tis so,'
When it proved otherwise?

KING. Not that I know.

POL. [*Pointing to his head and shoulder*] Take this from this, if this be otherwise.
If circumstances lead me, I will find
Where truth is hid, though it were hid indeed
Within the centre.[30]

KING. How may we try it further?

POL. You know, sometimes he walks four hours together
Here in the lobby.

QUEEN. So he does, indeed.

POL. At such a time I'll loose my daughter to him.
Be you and I behind an arras[31] then;
Mark the encounter. If he love her not,
And be not from his reason fall'n thereon,[32]
Let me be no assistant for a state,
But keep a farm and carters.

KING. We will try it.

QUEEN. But look where sadly the poor wretch comes reading.

POL. Away, I do beseech you both, away.
I'll board[33] him presently.[34] O, give me leave.
[*Exeunt* KING, QUEEN, *and* Attendants.

Enter HAMLET, *reading.*

How does my good Lord Hamlet?

HAM. Well, God-a-mercy.

POL. Do you know me, my lord?

HAM. Excellent well. You are a fishmonger.

POL. Not I, my lord.

[28] *lightness*] lightheadedness, mental derangement.
[29] *declension*] deterioration.
[30] *centre*] i.e., of the earth.
[31] *arras*] tapestry, named after the French town of Arras.
[32] *thereon*] on that account.
[33] *board*] accost, address.
[34] *presently*] immediately.

HAM. Then I would you were so honest a man.

POL. Honest, my lord?

HAM. Ay, sir. To be honest, as this world goes, is to be one man picked out of ten thousand.

POL. That's very true, my lord.

HAM. For if the sun breed maggots in a dead dog, being a good kissing carrion[35]—Have you a daughter?

POL. I have, my lord.

HAM. Let her not walk i' the sun. Conception[36] is a blessing, but as your daughter may conceive—friend, look to't.

POL. [*Aside*] How say you by that? Still[37] harping on my daughter. Yet he knew me not at first; he said I was a fishmonger. He is far gone. And truly in my youth I suffered much extremity for love, very near this. I'll speak to him again.—What do you read, my lord?

HAM. Words, words, words.

POL. What is the matter, my lord?

HAM. Between who?

POL. I mean, the matter that you read, my lord.

HAM. Slanders, sir. For the satirical rogue says here that old men have grey beards, that their faces are wrinkled, their eyes purging[38] thick amber and plum-tree gum, and that they have a plentiful lack of wit, together with most weak hams—all which, sir, though I most powerfully and potently believe, yet I hold it not honesty[39] to have it thus set down; for yourself, sir, shall grow old as I am, if like a crab you could go backward.

POL. [*Aside*] Though this be madness, yet there is method in't.—Will you walk out of the air, my lord?

HAM. Into my grave?

POL. Indeed, that's out of the air. [*Aside*] How pregnant sometimes his replies are!—a happiness that often madness hits on, which reason and sanity could not so prosperously be delivered of. I will leave him, and suddenly[40] contrive the means of meeting between him and my daughter.—My honourable lord, I will take my leave of you.

[35] *a good kissing carrion*] carrion good for kissing. "Carrion" can also have the meaning "live flesh."

[36] *Conception*] (1) forming concepts; (2) becoming pregnant.

[37] *Still*] always.

[38] *purging*] discharging.

[39] *honesty*] decency.

[40] *suddenly*] immediately.

HAM. You cannot, sir, take from me anything that I will more willingly part withal—except my life, except my life, except my life.

POL. Fare you well, my lord.

HAM. These tedious old fools!

Enter ROSENCRANTZ *and* GUILDENSTERN.

POL. You go to seek the Lord Hamlet. There he is.

ROS. [*To Polonius*] God save you, sir. [*Exit* POLONIUS.

GUIL. My honoured lord.

ROS. My most dear lord.

HAM. My excellent good friends. How dost thou, Guildenstern? Ah, Rosencrantz. Good lads, how do you both?

ROS. As the indifferent[41] children of the earth.

GUIL. Happy, in that we are not over-happy; on Fortune's cap we are not the very button.

HAM. Nor the soles of her shoe?

ROS. Neither, my lord.

HAM. Then you live about her waist, or in the middle of her favours?

GUIL. Faith, her privates[42] we.

HAM. In the secret parts of Fortune? O, most true; she is a strumpet. What's the news?

ROS. None, my lord, but that the world's grown honest.

HAM. Then is doomsday near. But your news is not true. Let me question more in particular. What have you, my good friends, deserved at the hands of Fortune that she sends you to prison hither?

GUIL. Prison, my lord?

HAM. Denmark's a prison.

ROS. Then is the world one.

HAM. A goodly one, in which there are many confines, wards and dungeons, Denmark being one o' the worst.

ROS. We think not so, my lord.

HAM. Why, then 'tis none to you; for there is nothing either good or bad but thinking makes it so. To me it is a prison.

ROS. Why, then your ambition makes it one: 'tis too narrow for your mind.

HAM. O God, I could be bounded in a nutshell and count myself a king of infinite space were it not that I have bad dreams.

[41] *indifferent*] ordinary.

[42] *privates*] (1) persons not holding a public office; (2) genitalia.

GUIL. Which dreams indeed are ambition; for the very substance of the ambitious is merely the shadow of a dream.

HAM. A dream itself is but a shadow.

ROS. Truly, and I hold ambition of so airy and light a quality that it is but a shadow's shadow.

HAM. Then are our beggars bodies, and our monarchs and outstretched heroes the beggars' shadows. Shall we to the court? For, by my fay, I cannot reason.

ROS. }
GUIL. } We'll wait upon[43] you.

HAM. No such matter. I will not sort[44] you with the rest of my servants; for, to speak to you like an honest man, I am most dreadfully attended. But, in the beaten way of friendship,[45] what make you at Elsinore?

ROS. To visit you, my lord, no other occasion.

HAM. Beggar that I am, I am even poor in thanks, but I thank you. And sure, dear friends, my thanks are too dear a halfpenny. Were you not sent for? Is it your own inclining? Is it a free visitation? Come, deal justly with me. Come, come. Nay, speak.

GUIL. What should we say, my lord?

HAM. Why, anything, but to the purpose. You were sent for; and there is a kind of confession in your looks which your modesties have not craft enough to colour. I know the good King and Queen have sent for you.

ROS. To what end, my lord?

HAM. That you must teach me. But let me conjure[46] you by the rights of our fellowship, by the consonancy of our youth, by the obligation of our ever-preserved love, and by what more dear a better proposer could charge you withal, be even[47] and direct with me whether you were sent for or no.

ROS. [*Aside to* GUIL.] What say you?

HAM. [*Aside*] Nay then, I have an eye of[48] you.—If you love me, hold not off.

GUIL. My lord, we were sent for.

HAM. I will tell you why. So shall my anticipation prevent your discovery,[49] and your secrecy to the King and Queen moult

[43] *wait upon*] escort.
[44] *sort*] class.
[45] *in the . . . friendship*] in the kind of plain language used among friends.
[46] *conjure*] entreat.
[47] *even*] honest.
[48] *of*] on.
[49] *prevent your discovery*] forestall your confession.

no feather. I have of late—but wherefore I know not—lost all my mirth, forgone all custom of exercises, and indeed it goes so heavily with my disposition that this goodly frame,[50] the earth, seems to me a sterile promontory. This most excellent canopy, the air, look you, this brave[51] o'erhanging firmament, this majestical roof fretted[52] with golden fire, why, it appears no other thing to me than a foul and pestilent congregation of vapours. What a piece of work is a man! How noble in reason, how infinite in faculty, in form and moving how express and admirable, in action how like an angel, in apprehension how like a god—the beauty of the world, the paragon of animals! And yet, to me, what is this quintessence of dust? Man delights not me—no, nor woman neither, though by your smiling you seem to say so.

ROS. My lord, there was no such stuff in my thoughts.

HAM. Why did you laugh then, when I said man delights not me?

ROS. To think, my lord, if you delight not in man, what lenten entertainment[53] the players shall receive from you. We coted[54] them on the way, and hither are they coming to offer you service.

HAM. He that plays the king shall be welcome; his Majesty shall have tribute of me. The adventurous knight shall use his foil and target,[55] the lover shall not sigh gratis, the humorous man[56] shall end his part in peace, the clown shall make those laugh whose lungs are tickle o' the sere,[57] and the lady shall say her mind freely, or the blank verse shall halt for't. What players are they?

ROS. Even those you were wont to take such delight in, the tragedians of the city.

HAM. How chances it they travel? Their residence, both in reputation and profit, was better both ways.

ROS. I think their inhibition[58] comes by the means of the late innovation.

[50] *frame*] structure.

[51] *brave*] beautiful.

[52] *fretted*] adorned.

[53] *lenten entertainment*] poor reception.

[54] *coted*] passed by.

[55] *foil and target*] fencing sword and targe (light shield)

[56] *humorous man*] stage character representing the effect of one of the four "humours," particularly that of "choler."

[57] *are tickle o' the sere*] have a hair trigger; i.e., will laugh at anything.

[58] *inhibition*] prohibition (from acting in the town).

HAM. Do they hold the same estimation they did when I was in the city? Are they so followed?

ROS. No, indeed, are they not.

HAM. How comes it? Do they grow rusty?

ROS. Nay, their endeavour keeps in the wonted pace. But there is, sir, an eyrie of children, little eyases,[59] that cry out on the top of question and are most tyrannically[60] clapped for't. These are now the fashion, and so berattle the common stages[61]—so they call them—that many wearing rapiers are afraid of goose-quills,[62] and dare scarce come thither.

HAM. What, are they children? Who maintains 'em? How are they escoted?[63] Will they pursue the quality[64] no longer than they can sing? Will they not say afterwards, if they should grow themselves to common players—as it is most like, if their means are no better—their writers do them wrong to make them exclaim against their own succession?[65]

ROS. Faith, there has been much to do on both sides, and the nation holds it no sin to tarre[66] them to controversy. There was for a while no money bid for argument[67] unless the poet and the player went to cuffs[68] in the question.[69]

HAM. Is't possible?

GUIL. O, there has been much throwing about of brains.

HAM. Do the boys carry it away?[70]

ROS. Ay, that they do, my lord, Hercules and his load[71] too.

HAM. It is not very strange; for my uncle is King of Denmark, and those that would make mows[72] at him while my father lived, give twenty, forty, fifty, a hundred ducats apiece for his picture in little. 'Sblood, there is something in this more than natural, if philosophy could find it out.

[*Flourish of trumpets within.*

[59] *eyases*] young hawks.
[60] *tyrannically*] violently.
[61] *berattle the common stages*] berate the public playhouses.
[62] *many . . . goose-quills*] gallants are afraid of being satirized.
[63] *escoted*] supported.
[64] *quality*] (acting) profession.
[65] *succession*] i.e., future profession.
[66] *tarre*] incite.
[67] *argument*] plots for plays.
[68] *went to cuffs*] attacked one another.
[69] *in the question*] concerning the controversy.
[70] *carry it away*] win.
[71] *Hercules and his load*] perhaps a reference to the Globe theatre, the sign of which portrayed Hercules supporting the earth.
[72] *mows*] faces.

GUIL. There are the players.

HAM. Gentlemen, you are welcome to Elsinore. Your hands, come then. The appurtenance of welcome is fashion and ceremony. Let me comply with you in this garb,[73] lest my extent[74] to the players—which, I tell you, must show fairly outwards—should more appear like entertainment than yours. You are welcome. But my uncle-father and aunt-mother are deceived.

GUIL. In what, my dear lord?

HAM. I am but mad north-north-west. When the wind is southerly I know a hawk from a handsaw.

Enter POLONIUS.

POL. Well be with you, gentlemen.

HAM. Hark you, Guildenstern, and you too—at each ear a hearer. That great baby you see there is not yet out of his swaddling clouts.

ROS. Happily[75] he's the second time come to them; for they say an old man is twice a child.

HAM. I will prophesy he comes to tell me of the players. Mark it. You say right, sir; o' Monday morning; 'twas so, indeed.

POL. My lord, I have news to tell you.

HAM. My lord, I have news to tell you. When Roscius[76] was an actor in Rome—

POL. The actors are come hither, my lord.

HAM. Buzz, buzz.

POL. Upon my honour—

HAM. Then came each actor on his ass—

POL. The best actors in the world, either for tragedy, comedy, history, pastoral, pastoral-comical, historical-pastoral, tragical-historical, tragical-comical-historical-pastoral, scene individable,[77] or poem unlimited.[78] Seneca cannot be too heavy, nor Plautus too light. For the law of writ and the liberty, these are the only men.

HAM. O Jephthah, judge of Israel,[79] what a treasure hadst thou!

POL. What a treasure had he, my lord?

[73] *garb*] manner.
[74] *extent*] welcome.
[75] *Happily*] haply, perhaps.
[76] *Roscius*] the most celebrated actor of ancient Rome.
[77] *individable*] unclassifiable.
[78] *unlimited*] undefined.
[79] *Jephthah, judge of Israel*] a Biblical figure who sacrificed his own daughter.

HAM. Why,

> One fair daughter, and no more,
> The which he loved passing[80] well.

POL. [*Aside*] Still on my daughter.

HAM. Am I not i' the right, old Jephthah?

POL. If you call me Jephthah, my lord, I have a daughter that I love passing well.

HAM. Nay, that follows not.

POL. What follows, then, my lord?

HAM. Why,

> As by lot God wot,

and then, you know,

> It came to pass, as most like it was—

The first row[81] of the pious chanson will show you more; for look where my abridgement[82] comes.

Enter the Players.

You are welcome, masters. Welcome, all. I am glad to see thee well. Welcome, good friends. O, my old friend! Why, thy face is valanced[83] since I saw thee last. Comest thou to beard[84] me in Denmark? What, my young lady[85] and mistress! By'r lady, your ladyship is nearer to heaven than when I saw you last, by the altitude of a chopine.[86] Pray God, your voice, like a piece of uncurrent gold, be not cracked within the ring.[87] Masters, you are all welcome. We'll e'en to't like French falconers, fly at any thing we see.[88] We'll have a speech straight. Come, give us a taste of your quality. Come, a passionate speech.

FIRST PLAY. What speech, my good lord?

[80] *passing*] exceedingly.

[81] *row*] stanza.

[82] *abridgement*] (1) entertainment; (2) reason for cutting short the conversation with Polonius.

[83] *valanced*] fringed (bearded).

[84] *beard*] face, defy (with the obvious pun on the actor's new facial hair).

[85] *my young lady*] a boy who would play a woman's role.

[86] *chopine*] a woman's thick-soled shoe.

[87] *cracked within the ring*] A coin that had been clipped within the ring surrounding the sovereign's head was not legal tender.

[88] *French . . . see*] Falcons were trained to attack only one kind of quarry. Hamlet is thus expressing his overenthusiasm.

HAM. I heard thee speak me a speech once, but it was never acted, or, if it was, not above once; for the play, I remember, pleased not the million, 'twas caviare to the general.[89] But it was—as I received it, and others, whose judgements in such matters cried in the top of[90] mine—an excellent play, well digested[91] in the scenes, set down with as much modesty[92] as cunning.[93] I remember, one said there were no sallets[94] in the lines to make the matter savoury, nor no matter in the phrase that might indict the author of affection,[95] but called it an honest method, as wholesome as sweet, and by very much more handsome than fine. One speech in it I chiefly loved: 'twas Æneas' tale to Dido, and thereabout of it especially where he speaks of Priam's slaughter.[96] If it live in your memory, begin at this line—let me see, let me see—

The rugged Pyrrhus, like th' Hyrcanian beast—[97]
It is not so. It begins with Pyrrhus—
The rugged Pyrrhus, he whose sable arms,[98]
Black as his purpose, did the night resemble
When he lay couched in the ominous horse,[99]
Hath now this dread and black complexion smear'd
With heraldry more dismal. Head to foot
Now is he total gules,[100] horridly trick'd[101]
With blood of fathers, mothers, daughters, sons,
Baked and impasted with the parching streets,
That lend a tyrannous and a damned light
To their lord's murder. Roasted in wrath and fire,
And thus o'er-sized[102] with coagulate gore,
With eyes like carbuncles, the hellish Pyrrhus
Old grandsire Priam seeks.
So, proceed you.

[89] *caviare to the general*] i.e., too rich for common taste.
[90] *in the top of*] with more authority than.
[91] *digested*] arranged.
[92] *modesty*] restraint.
[93] *cunning*] skill.
[94] *sallets*] salad, relish; here, offensive language.
[95] *affection*] affectation.
[96] *Priam's slaughter*] for the account of the sacking of Troy, see Virgil's *Aeneid*, II.
[97] *Hyrcanian beast*] tiger (from Hyrcania, a region on the southeast coast of the Caspian sea).
[98] *sable arms*] black armor.
[99] *the ominous horse*] the Trojan horse.
[100] *gules*] a heraldic term for red.
[101] *trick'd*] a heraldic term; here, adorned.
[102] *o'ersized*] smeared.

POL. 'Fore God, my lord, well spoken, with good accent and good discretion.

FIRST PLAY. Anon he finds him
Striking too short at Greeks. His antique sword,
Rebellious to his arm, lies where it falls,
Repugnant[103] to command. Unequal match'd,
Pyrrhus at Priam drives, in rage strikes wide,
But with the whiff and wind of his fell[104] sword
The unnerved father falls. Then senseless[105] Ilium,
Seeming to feel this blow, with flaming top
Stoops to his base, and with a hideous crash
Takes prisoner Pyrrhus' ear. For, lo! his sword,
Which was declining on the milky head
Of reverend Priam, seem'd i' the air to stick.
So, as a painted tyrant, Pyrrhus stood,
And like a neutral to his will and matter,[106]
Did nothing.
But as we often see, against[107] some storm,
A silence in the heavens, the rack[108] stand still,
The bold winds speechless and the orb below
As hush as death, anon the dreadful thunder
Doth rend the region,[109] so after Pyrrhus' pause
Aroused vengeance[110] sets him new a-work,
And never did the Cyclops' hammers fall
On Mars's armour, forged for proof[111] eterne,
With less remorse[112] than Pyrrhus' bleeding sword
Now falls on Priam.
Out, out, thou strumpet, Fortune! All you gods,
In general synod take away her power,
Break all the spokes and fellies[113] from her wheel,
And bowl the round nave[114] down the hill of heaven
As low as to the fiends.

POL. This is too long.

[103] *Repugnant*] refractory.
[104] *fell*] fierce.
[105] *senseless*] insensate.
[106] *matter*] purpose, aim.
[107] *against*] before.
[108] *rack*] clouds.
[109] *region*] sky, air.
[110] *vengeance*] Achilles, Pyrrhus' father, had been killed by Paris, Priam's son.
[111] *proof*] tested and found impenetrable.
[112] *remorse*] compassion.
[113] *fellies*] rim.
[114] *nave*] hub.

HAM. It shall to the barber's, with your beard. Prithee, say on. He's for a jig[115] or a tale of bawdry, or he sleeps. Say on; come to Hecuba.

FIRST PLAY. But who, O, who had seen the mobled[116] queen—

HAM. 'The mobled queen?'

POL. That's good; 'mobled queen' is good.

FIRST PLAY. Run barefoot up and down, threatening the flames
With bisson rheum,[117] a clout upon that head
Where late the diadem stood, and for a robe,
About her lank and all o'er-teemed[118] loins,
A blanket, in the alarm of fear caught up;
Who this had seen, with tongue in venom steep'd
'Gainst Fortune's state would treason have pronounced.
But if the gods themselves did see her then,
When she saw Pyrrhus make malicious sport
In mincing with his sword her husband's limbs,
The instant burst of clamour that she made,
Unless things mortal move them not at all,
Would have made milch[119] the burning eyes of heaven
And passion in the gods.

POL. Look whether he has not turned his colour and has tears in's eyes. Prithee, no more.

HAM. 'Tis well. I'll have thee speak out the rest of this soon. Good my lord, will you see the players well bestowed?[120] Do you hear, let them be well used, for they are the abstract[121] and brief chronicles of the time. After your death you were better have a bad epitaph than their ill report while you live.

POL. My lord, I will use them according to their desert.

HAM. God's bodykins, man, much better. Use every man after his desert, and who shall 'scape whipping? Use them after your own honour and dignity: the less they deserve, the more merit is in your bounty. Take them in.

POL. Come, sirs.

HAM. Follow him, friends. We'll hear a play tomorrow.

[*Exit* POLONIUS *with all the* Players *but the* First.]

Dost thou hear me, old friend? Can you play *The Murder of Gonzago*?

[115] *jig*] a farcical metrical composition with singing and dancing.
[116] *mobled*] with head muffled.
[117] *bisson rheum*] blinding tears.
[118] *o'er-teemed*] worn out by childbearing.
[119] *milch*] shed milky tears.
[120] *bestowed*] lodged.
[121] *abstract*] summary.

FIRST PLAY. Ay, my lord.

HAM. We'll ha't tomorrow night. You could, for a need,[122] study a speech of some dozen or sixteen lines, which I would set down and insert in't, could you not?

FIRST PLAY. Ay, my lord.

HAM. Very well. Follow that lord, and look you mock him not. [*Exit* FIRST PLAYER.] My good friends, I'll leave you till night. You are welcome to Elsinore.

ROS. Good my lord.

HAM. Ay, so. God be wi' ye.

[*Exeunt* ROSENCRANTZ *and* GUILDENSTERN.

Now I am alone.
O, what a rogue and peasant slave am I!
Is it not monstrous that this player here,
But in a fiction, in a dream of passion,
Could force his soul so to his own conceit
That from her working all his visage wann'd,
Tears in his eyes, distraction in's aspect,
A broken voice, and his whole function suiting
With forms to his conceit?[123] And all for nothing!
For Hecuba!
What's Hecuba to him, or he to Hecuba,
That he should weep for her? What would he do,
Had he the motive and the cue for passion
That I have? He would drown the stage with tears
And cleave the general ear with horrid speech,
Make mad the guilty and appal the free,[124]
Confound the ignorant, and amaze[125] indeed
The very faculties of eyes and ears.
Yet I,
A dull and muddy-mettled[126] rascal, peak,[127]
Like John-a-dreams, unpregnant of[128] my cause,
And can say nothing; no, not for a king,
Upon whose property and most dear life
A damn'd defeat was made. Am I a coward?
Who calls me villain, breaks my pate across,
Plucks off my beard and blows it in my face,

[122] *for a need*] if necessary.
[123] *his whole . . . conceit*] his entire being producing gestures to match his conception.
[124] *free*] innocent.
[125] *amaze*] confuse.
[126] *muddy-mettled*] dull-spirited.
[127] *peak*] mope.
[128] *unpregnant of*] indifferent to.

Tweaks me by the nose, gives me the lie i' the throat,
As deep as to the lungs? Who does me this?
Ha!
'Swounds, I should take it: for it cannot be
But I am pigeon-liver'd and lack gall
To make oppression bitter,[129] or ere this
I should have fatted all the region kites[130]
With this slave's offal. Bloody, bawdy villain!
Remorseless, treacherous, lecherous, kindless[131] villain!
Why, what an ass am I! This is most brave,
That I, the son of a dear father murder'd,
Prompted to my revenge by heaven and hell,
Must, like a whore, unpack my heart with words,
And fall a-cursing, like a very drab,[132]
A scullion![133] Fie upon't! Foh!
About,[134] my brain! Hum, I have heard
That guilty creatures, sitting at a play,
Have by the very cunning of the scene
Been struck so to the soul that presently[135]
They have proclaim'd their malefactions.
For murder, though it have no tongue, will speak
With most miraculous organ. I'll have these players
Play something like the murder of my father
Before mine uncle. I'll observe his looks,
I'll tent[136] him to the quick. If he but blench,[137]
I know my course. The spirit that I have seen
May be the devil, and the devil hath power
To assume a pleasing shape, yea, and perhaps
Out of my weakness and my melancholy,
As he is very potent with such spirits,[138]
Abuses me to damn me. I'll have grounds
More relative[139] than this. The play's the thing
Wherein I'll catch the conscience of the King. [*Exit.*

[129] *pigeon-liver'd . . . bitter*] Pigeons were thought not to produce gall, and therefore to be without malice.
[130] *region kites*] kites of the air.
[131] *kindless*] unnatural.
[132] *drab*] prostitute.
[133] *scullion*] kitchen servant.
[134] *About*] get active.
[135] *presently*] immediately.
[136] *tent*] probe, search.
[137] *blench*] start, flinch.
[138] *spirits*] humors.
[139] *relative*] to the purpose, conclusive.

ACT III.

SCENE I. *A room in the castle.*

Enter KING, QUEEN, POLONIUS, OPHELIA, ROSENCRANTZ, *and* GUILDENSTERN.

KING. And can you by no drift of conference[1]
Get from him why he puts on this confusion,
Grating so harshly all his days of quiet
With turbulent and dangerous lunacy?

ROS. He does confess he feels himself distracted,
But from what cause he will by no means speak.

GUIL. Nor do we find him forward to be sounded;
But, with a crafty madness, keeps aloof,
When we would bring him on to some confession
Of his true state.

QUEEN. Did he receive you well?

ROS. Most like a gentleman.

GUIL. But with much forcing of his disposition.

ROS. Niggard of question,[2] but of our demands
Most free in his reply.

QUEEN. Did you assay him
To any pastime?[3]

ROS. Madam, it so fell out that certain players
We o'er-raught[4] on the way. Of these we told him,
And there did seem in him a kind of joy
To hear of it. They are about the court,
And, as I think, they have already order

[1] *drift of conference*] turn of conversation.
[2] *Niggard of question*] sparing in conversation.
[3] *assay . . . pastime*] tempt him with any form of entertainment.
[4] *o'er-raught*] overtook.

This night to play before him.

POL. 'Tis most true;
And he beseech'd me to entreat your Majesties
To hear and see the matter.

KING. With all my heart; and it doth much content me
To hear him so inclined.
Good gentlemen, give him a further edge,[5]
And drive his purpose on to these delights.

ROS. We shall, my lord.

[*Exeunt* ROSENCRANTZ *and* GUILDENSTERN.

KING. Sweet Gertrude, leave us too;
For we have closely[6] sent for Hamlet hither,
That he, as 'twere by accident, may here
Affront[7] Ophelia.
Her father and myself, lawful espials,[8]
Will so bestow ourselves that, seeing unseen,
We may of their encounter frankly judge,
And gather by him, as he is behaved,
If't be the affliction of his love or no
That thus he suffers for.

QUEEN. I shall obey you.
And for your part, Ophelia, I do wish
That your good beauties be the happy cause
Of Hamlet's wildness; so shall I hope your virtues
Will bring him to his wonted way again,
To both your honours.

OPH. Madam, I wish it may. [*Exit* QUEEN.

POL. Ophelia, walk you here. Gracious,[9] so please you,
We will bestow ourselves. [*To* OPHELIA.] Read on this book,
That show of such an exercise[10] may colour
Your loneliness.[11] We are oft to blame in this—
'Tis too much proved—that with devotion's visage
And pious action we do sugar o'er
The devil himself.

KING. [*Aside*] O, 'tis too true.

[5] *edge*] incitement.
[6] *closely*] secretly.
[7] *Affront*] encounter.
[8] *espials*] spies.
[9] *Gracious*] Your Grace.
[10] *exercise*] act of religious devotion.
[11] *colour Your loneliness*] make your being alone seem plausible.

How smart a lash that speech doth give my conscience.
The harlot's cheek, beautied with plastering art,
Is not more ugly to the thing that helps it
Than is my deed to my most painted word.
O heavy burden!

POL. I hear him coming. Let's withdraw, my lord.
[*Exeunt* KING *and* POLONIUS.

Enter HAMLET.

HAM. To be, or not to be, that is the question:
Whether 'tis nobler in the mind to suffer
The slings and arrows of outrageous fortune,
Or to take arms against a sea of troubles,
And by opposing end them. To die: to sleep;
No more; and by a sleep to say we end
The heart-ache and the thousand natural shocks
That flesh is heir to; 'tis a consummation
Devoutly to be wish'd. To die, to sleep;
To sleep; perchance to dream. Ay, there's the rub;[12]
For in that sleep of death what dreams may come,
When we have shuffled off[13] this mortal coil,[14]
Must give us pause—there's the respect
That makes calamity of so long life.[15]
For who would bear the whips and scorns of time,
The oppressor's wrong, the proud man's contumely,
The pangs of disprized[16] love, the law's delay,
The insolence of office, and the spurns
That patient merit of the unworthy takes,
When he himself might his quietus[17] make
With a bare bodkin?[18] Who would fardels[19] bear,
To grunt and sweat under a weary life,
But that the dread of something after death,
The undiscover'd country from whose bourn[20]
No traveller returns, puzzles the will,

[12] *rub*] obstacle (a bowling term for anything blocking or deflecting the course of the bowl).
[13] *shuffled off*] cast off.
[14] *coil*] (1) turmoil; (2) (?) rope.
[15] *of so long life*] so long-lived.
[16] *disprized*] undervalued.
[17] *quietus*] final settlement of an account.
[18] *bare bodkin*] mere dagger.
[19] *fardels*] burdens, packs.
[20] *bourn*] boundary.

And makes us rather bear those ills we have
Than fly to others that we know not of?
Thus conscience[21] does make cowards of us all,
And thus the native hue of resolution
Is sicklied o'er with the pale cast of thought,
And enterprises of great pitch[22] and moment
With this regard their currents turn awry
And lose the name of action. Soft you now,
The fair Ophelia! Nymph, in thy orisons[23]
Be all my sins remember'd.

OPH. Good my lord,
How does your honour for this many a day?

HAM. I humbly thank you: well.

OPH. My lord, I have remembrances of yours
That I have longed long to redeliver.
I pray you, now receive them.

HAM. No, not I.
I never gave you aught.

OPH. My honour'd lord, you know right well you did;
And with them words of so sweet breath composed
As made the things more rich. Their perfume lost,
Take these again; for to the noble mind
Rich gifts wax poor when givers prove unkind.
There, my lord.

HAM. Ha, ha! Are you honest?[24]

OPH. My lord?

HAM. Are you fair?

OPH. What means your lordship?

HAM. That if you be honest and fair, your honesty should admit no discourse to your beauty.

OPH. Could beauty, my lord, have better commerce than with honesty?

HAM. Ay, truly; for the power of beauty will sooner transform honesty from what it is to a bawd than the force of honesty can translate beauty into his likeness. This was sometime a paradox, but now the time gives it proof. I did love you once.

OPH. Indeed, my lord, you made me believe so.

[21] *conscience*] (1) consciousness; (2) conscience.
[22] *pitch*] height.
[23] *orisons*] prayers.
[24] *honest*] (1) truthful; (2) chaste.

HAM. You should not have believed me; for virtue cannot so inoculate[25] our old stock but we shall relish of it.[26] I loved you not.

OPH. I was the more deceived.

HAM. Get thee to a nunnery. Why, wouldst thou be a breeder of sinners? I am myself indifferent[27] honest, but yet I could accuse me of such things that it were better my mother had not borne me. I am very proud, revengeful, ambitious, with more offences at my beck[28] than I have thoughts to put them in, imagination to give them shape, or time to act them in. What should such fellows as I do crawling between heaven and earth? We are arrant knaves all. Believe none of us. Go thy ways to a nunnery. Where's your father?

OPH. At home, my lord.

HAM. Let the doors be shut upon him, that he may play the fool nowhere but in's own house. Farewell.

OPH. O, help him, you sweet heavens!

HAM. If thou dost marry, I'll give thee this plague for thy dowry: be thou as chaste as ice, as pure as snow, thou shalt not escape calumny. Get thee to a nunnery, farewell. Or, if thou wilt needs marry, marry a fool; for wise men know well enough what monsters[29] you make of them. To a nunnery, go; and quickly too. Farewell.

OPH. O heavenly powers, restore him!

HAM. I have heard of your paintings too, well enough. God hath given you one face, and you make yourselves another. You jig, you amble, and you lisp, and nickname God's creatures, and make your wantonness your ignorance. Go to, I'll no more on't; it hath made me mad. I say, we will have no more marriages. Those that are married already—all but one—shall live; the rest shall keep as they are. To a nunnery, go. [*Exit.*

OPH. O, what a noble mind is here o'erthrown!
The courtier's, soldier's, scholar's, eye, tongue, sword,
The expectancy and rose of the fair state,
The glass of fashion and the mould of form,
The observed[30] of all observers, quite, quite down!
And I, of ladies most deject and wretched,

[25] *inoculate*] graft.
[26] *of it*] i.e., of the old, sinful nature.
[27] *indifferent*] moderately.
[28] *at my beck*] ready to be committed.
[29] *monsters*] i.e., cuckolds (having grown horns).
[30] *observed*] revered, respected.

That suck'd the honey of his music vows,
Now see that noble and most sovereign reason
Like sweet bells jangled out of tune and harsh,
That unmatch'd form and feature of blown[31] youth
Blasted with ecstasy.[32] O, woe is me,
To have seen what I have seen, see what I see!

Enter KING *and* POLONIUS.

KING. Love? His affections do not that way tend;
Nor what he spake, though it lack'd form a little,
Was not like madness. There's something in his soul
O'er which his melancholy sits on brood,
And I do doubt[33] the hatch and the disclose
Will be some danger; which for to prevent,
I have in quick determination
Thus set it down: he shall with speed to England,
For the demand of our neglected tribute.
Haply the seas and countries different
With variable objects shall expel
This something-settled matter in his heart,
Whereon his brains still[34] beating puts him thus
From fashion of himself.[35] What think you on't?

POL. It shall do well. But yet do I believe
The origin and commencement of his grief
Sprung from neglected love. How now, Ophelia?
You need not tell us what Lord Hamlet said;
We heard it all. My lord, do as you please;
But, if you hold it fit, after the play,
Let his queen mother all alone entreat him
To show his grief. Let her be round[36] with him;
And I'll be placed, so please you, in the ear
Of all their conference. If she find him not,
To England send him, or confine him where
Your wisdom best shall think.

KING. It shall be so.
Madness in great ones must not unwatch'd go. [*Exeunt*.

[31] *blown*] in full blossom.
[32] *ecstasy*] madness.
[33] *doubt*] fear.
[34] *still*] constantly.
[35] *From fashion of himself*] out of his normal manner.
[36] *be round*] speak plainly.

SCENE II. *A hall in the castle.*

Enter HAMLET *and* Players.

HAM. Speak the speech, I pray you, as I pronounced it to you, trippingly on the tongue. But if you mouth it, as many of your players do, I had as lief the town-crier spoke my lines. Nor do not saw the air too much with your hand, thus; but use all gently: for in the very torrent, tempest, and, as I may say, whirlwind of your passion, you must acquire and beget a temperance that may give it smoothness. O, it offends me to the soul to hear a robustious periwig-pated fellow tear a passion to tatters, to very rags, to split the ears of the groundlings,[1] who, for the most part, are capable of[2] nothing but inexplicable dumb-shows and noise. I would have such a fellow whipped for o'erdoing Termagant.[3] It out-Herods Herod.[4] Pray you, avoid it.

FIRST PLAY. I warrant your honour.

HAM. Be not too tame neither, but let your own discretion be your tutor. Suit the action to the word, the word to the action, with this special observance, that you o'erstep not the modesty of nature. For anything so overdone is from the purpose of playing, whose end, both at the first and now, was and is, to hold, as 'twere, the mirror up to nature, to show virtue her own feature, scorn her own image, and the very age and body of the time his form and pressure.[5] Now this overdone or come tardy off,[6] though it make the unskilful laugh, cannot but make the judicious grieve, the censure[7] of the which one must in your allowance o'erweigh a whole theatre of others. O, there be players that I have seen play, and heard others praise, and that highly, not to speak it profanely, that neither having the accent of Christians nor the

[1] *groundlings*] those spectators who stood in the pit of the theater.

[2] *capable of*] responsive to.

[3] *Termagant*] a legendary Muslim deity, presented as a violently noisy character in medieval dramas.

[4] *Herod*] Herod was presented as a ranting tyrant in medieval dramas.

[5] *pressure*] stamped impression.

[6] *come tardy off*] performed inadequately.

[7] *censure*] critical judgement.

gait of Christian, pagan, nor man, have so strutted and bellowed, that I have thought some of Nature's journeymen[8] had made men, and not made them well, they imitated humanity so abominably.

FIRST PLAY. I hope we have reformed that indifferently[9] with us, sir.

HAM. O, reform it altogether. And let those that play your clowns speak no more than is set down for them; for there be of them that will themselves laugh, to set on some quantity of barren spectators to laugh too, though in the meantime some necessary question of the play be then to be considered. That's villanous, and shows a most pitiful ambition in the fool that uses it. Go, make you ready. [*Exeunt* Players.

Enter POLONIUS, ROSENCRANTZ, *and* GUILDENSTERN.

How now, my lord! Will the King hear this piece of work?

POL. And the Queen too, and that presently.[10]

HAM. Bid the players make haste. [*Exit* POLONIUS.
Will you two help to hasten them?

ROS.
GUIL. } We will, my lord.

[*Exeunt* ROSENCRANTZ *and* GUILDENSTERN.

HAM. What ho, Horatio!

Enter HORATIO.

HOR. Here, sweet lord, at your service.

HAM. Horatio, thou art e'en as just a man
As e'er my conversation coped[11] withal.

HOR. O, my dear lord—

HAM. Nay, do not think I flatter;
For what advancement may I hope from thee,
That no revenue hast but thy good spirits,
To feed and clothe thee? Why should the poor be flatter'd?
No, let the candied tongue lick absurd[12] pomp,
And crook the pregnant[13] hinges of the knee
Where thrift[14] may follow fawning. Dost thou hear?

[8] *journeymen*] hired workmen.
[9] *indifferently*] tolerably well.
[10] *presently*] immediately.
[11] *coped*] encountered.
[12] *absurd*] insipid.
[13] *pregnant*] ready.
[14] *thrift*] profit.

Since my dear soul was mistress of her choice,
And could of men distinguish her election,
Sh'hath seal'd thee for herself; for thou hast been
As one, in suffering all, that suffers nothing,
A man that Fortune's buffets and rewards
Hast ta'en with equal thanks; and blest are those
Whose blood[15] and judgement are so well commeddled[16]
That they are not a pipe for Fortune's finger
To sound what stop she please. Give me that man
That is not passion's slave, and I will wear him
In my heart's core, ay, in my heart of heart,
As I do thee. Something too much of this.
There is a play tonight before the King.
One scene of it comes near the circumstance
Which I have told thee of my father's death.
I prithee, when thou seest that act afoot,
Even with the very comment[17] of thy soul
Observe my uncle. If his occulted guilt
Do not itself unkennel in one speech,
It is a damned ghost that we have seen,
And my imaginations are as foul
As Vulcan's stithy.[18] Give him heedful note;
For I mine eyes will rivet to his face,
And after we will both our judgements join
In censure of his seeming.[19]

HOR. Well, my lord.
If he steal aught the whilst this play is playing,
And 'scape detecting, I will pay the theft.

HAM. They are coming to the play. I must be idle.[20]
Get you a place.

Danish march. A flourish. Enter KING, QUEEN, POLONIUS, OPHELIA, ROSENCRANTZ, GUILDENSTERN, *and other Lords attendant, with the Guard carrying torches.*

KING. How fares our cousin Hamlet?

[15] *blood*] passion.
[16] *commeddled*] commingled.
[17] *the very comment*] the most searching judgment.
[18] *Vulcan's stithy*] the smithy of Vulcan, god of fire and metalworking.
[19] *In censure of his seeming*] in judgment of his behavior.
[20] *idle*] unoccupied, distracted.

HAM. Excellent, i' faith; of the chameleon's dish.[21] I eat the air, promise-crammed. You cannot feed capons so.

KING. I have nothing with this answer, Hamlet. These words are not mine.[22]

HAM. No, nor mine now. [*To* POLONIUS] My lord, you played once i' the university, you say?

POL. That did I, my lord, and was accounted a good actor.

HAM. What did you enact?

POL. I did enact Julius Cæsar. I was killed i' the Capitol. Brutus killed me.

HAM. It was a brute part of him to kill so capital a calf there. Be the players ready?

ROS. Ay, my lord; they stay upon your patience.

QUEEN. Come hither, my dear Hamlet, sit by me.

HAM. No, good mother, here's metal more attractive.

POL. [*To the* KING] O, ho! do you mark that?

HAM. Lady, shall I lie in your lap? [*Lying down at* OPHELIA's *feet.*

OPH. No, my lord.

HAM. I mean, my head upon your lap?

OPH. Ay, my lord.

HAM. Do you think I meant country matters?

OPH. I think nothing, my lord.

HAM. That's a fair thought to lie between maids' legs.

OPH. What is, my lord?

HAM. Nothing.

OPH. You are merry, my lord.

HAM. Who, I?

OPH. Ay, my lord.

HAM. O God, your only jig-maker. What should a man do but be merry? For, look you, how cheerfully my mother looks, and my father died within's two hours.

OPH. Nay, 'tis twice two months, my lord.

HAM. So long? Nay then, let the devil wear black, for I'll have a suit of sables. O heavens, die two months ago, and not forgotten yet! Then there's hope a great man's memory may outlive his life half a year. But, by'r lady, he must build churches then, or else shall he suffer not thinking on, with the hobby-horse,[23] whose epitaph is, 'For, O, for, O, the hobby-horse is forgot.'

[21] *the chameleon's dish*] Chameleons were said to feed on air. Hamlet deliberately misinterprets "fare" to mean "feed."

[22] *are not mine*] do not correspond to my question.

[23] *hobby-horse*] a character in the morris dance.

Hautboys play. The dumb-show enters.

Enter a King *and a* Queen *very lovingly, the* Queen *embracing him, and he her. She kneels and makes show of protestation unto him. He takes her up and declines his head upon her neck; lays him down upon a bank of flowers. She, seeing him asleep, leaves him. Anon comes in a fellow, takes off his crown, kisses it, and pours poison in the* King's *ears, and exit. The* Queen *returns, finds the* King *dead, and makes passionate action. The* Poisoner, *with some two or three* Mutes, *comes in again, seeming to lament with her. The dead body is carried away. The* Poisoner *wooes the* Queen *with gifts. She seems loath and unwilling awhile, but in the end accepts his love.* [*Exeunt.*

OPH. What means this, my lord?
HAM. Marry, this is miching mallecho.[24] It means mischief.
OPH. Belike this show imports the argument[25] of the play.

Enter PROLOGUE.

HAM. We shall know by this fellow. The players cannot keep counsel; they'll tell all.
OPH. Will he tell us what this show meant?
HAM. Ay, or any show that you'll show him. Be not you ashamed to show, he'll not shame to tell you what it means.
OPH. You are naught,[26] you are naught. I'll mark the play.
PRO. For us, and for our tragedy,
Here stooping to your clemency,
We beg your hearing patiently.
HAM. Is this a prologue, or the posy[27] of a ring?
OPH. 'Tis brief, my lord.
HAM. As woman's love.

Enter two Players, KING *and* QUEEN.

P. KING. Full thirty times hath Phœbus' cart[28] gone round
Neptune's salt wash and Tellus' orbed ground,[29]
And thirty dozen moons with borrowed sheen
About the world have times twelve thirties been,
Since love our hearts and Hymen[30] did our hands
Unite commutual in most sacred bands.

[24] *miching mallecho*] insidious mischief.
[25] *argument*] plot.
[26] *naught*] worthless, indecent.
[27] *posy*] a motto inscribed on a ring.
[28] *Phœbus' cart*] the chariot of the sun-god.
[29] *Tellus' orbed ground*] the earth.
[30] *Hymen*] the god of marriage.

P. QUEEN. So many journeys may the sun and moon
Make us again count o'er ere love be done.
But, woe is me, you are so sick of late,
So far from cheer and from your former state,
That I distrust[31] you. Yet, though I distrust,
Discomfort you, my lord, it nothing must.
For women's fear and love hold quantity,[32]
In neither aught, or in extremity.
Now, what my love is, proof hath made you know,
And as my love is sized, my fear is so.
Where love is great, the littlest doubts are fear,
Where little fears grow great, great love grows there.
P. KING. Faith, I must leave thee, love, and shortly too.
My operant[33] powers their functions leave to do,[34]
And thou shalt live in this fair world behind,
Honour'd, beloved; and haply one as kind
For husband shalt thou—
P. QUEEN. O, confound the rest!
Such love must needs be treason in my breast.
In second husband let me be accurst,
None wed the second but who kill'd the first.
HAM. [*Aside*] Wormwood, wormwood.
P. QUEEN. The instances[35] that second marriage move
Are base respects of thrift,[36] but none of love.
A second time I kill my husband dead
When second husband kisses me in bed.
P. KING. I do believe you think what now you speak,
But what we do determine oft we break.
Purpose is but the slave to memory,
Of violent birth but poor validity,
Which now, like fruit unripe, sticks on the tree,
But fall unshaken when they mellow be.
Most necessary 'tis that we forget
To pay ourselves what to ourselves is debt.
What to ourselves in passion we propose,
The passion ending, doth the purpose lose.

[31] *distrust*] feel concern for.
[32] *hold quantity*] are in proportion to one another.
[33] *operant*] active.
[34] *leave to do*] cease to carry out.
[35] *instances*] motives.
[36] *thrift*] profit, gain.

The violence of either grief or joy
Their own enactures[37] with themselves destroy.
Where joy most revels, grief doth most lament;
Grief joys, joy grieves, on slender accident.
This world is not for aye, nor 'tis not strange
That even our loves should with our fortunes change,
For 'tis a question left us yet to prove,
Whether love lead fortune or else fortune love.
The great man down, you mark his favourite flies,
The poor advanced makes friends of enemies.
And hitherto doth love on fortune tend;
For who not needs shall never lack a friend,
And who in want a hollow friend doth try
Directly seasons him[38] his enemy.
But, orderly to end where I begun,
Our wills and fates do so contrary run,
That our devices still[39] are overthrown;
Our thoughts are ours, their ends none of our own.
So think thou wilt no second husband wed,
But die thy thoughts when thy first lord is dead.

P. QUEEN. Nor earth to me give food nor heaven light,
Sport and repose lock from me day and night,
To desperation turn my trust and hope,
An anchor's cheer[40] in prison be my scope,
Each opposite, that blanks[41] the face of joy,
Meet what I would have well and it destroy,
Both here and hence pursue me lasting strife,
If, once a widow, ever I be wife.

HAM. If she should break it now.

P. KING. 'Tis deeply sworn. Sweet, leave me here awhile.
My spirits grow dull, and fain I would beguile
The tedious day with sleep. [*Sleeps.*

P. QUEEN. Sleep rock thy brain,
And never come mischance between us twain. [*Exit.*

HAM. Madam, how like you this play?

QUEEN. The lady doth protest too much, methinks.

HAM. O, but she'll keep her word.

[37] *enactures*] fulfillments.
[38] *seasons him*] ripens him into.
[39] *still*] always.
[40] *anchor's cheer*] anchorite's fare.
[41] *blanks*] blanches, makes pale.

KING. Have you heard the argument? Is there no offence in't?

HAM. No, no, they do but jest, poison in jest. No offence i' the world.

KING. What do you call the play?

HAM. *The Mousetrap.* Marry, how? Tropically.[42] This play is the image of a murder done in Vienna. Gonzago is the Duke's name; his wife, Baptista. You shall see anon. 'Tis a knavish piece of work, but what o' that? Your Majesty, and we that have free[43] souls, it touches us not. Let the galled jade[44] wince, our withers are unwrung.[45]

Enter LUCIANUS.

This is one Lucianus, nephew to the King.

OPH. You are as good as a chorus, my lord.

HAM. I could interpret between you and your love, if I could see the puppets dallying.

OPH. You are keen,[46] my lord, you are keen.

HAM. It would cost you a groaning[47] to take off my edge.[48]

OPH. Still better, and worse.

HAM. So you mistake[49] your husbands. Begin, murderer. Pox, leave thy damnable faces and begin. Come, the croaking raven doth bellow for revenge.

LUC. Thoughts black, hands apt, drugs fit, and time agreeing,
Confederate season, else no creature seeing;
Thou mixture rank, of midnight weeds collected,
With Hecate's ban[50] thrice blasted, thrice infected,
Thy natural magic and dire property,
On wholesome life usurp[51] immediately.

[*Pours the poison into the sleeper's ear.*

HAM. He poisons him i' the garden for his estate. His name's Gonzago. The story is extant, and written in very choice Italian. You shall see anon how the murderer gets the love of Gonzago's wife.

OPH. The King rises.

[42] *Tropically*] metaphorically.
[43] *free*] innocent.
[44] *galled jade*] horse rubbed sore (by a saddle or harness).
[45] *unwrung*] not pinched.
[46] *keen*] bitter.
[47] *groaning*] i.e., sexual intercourse.
[48] *edge*] i.e., sexual appetite.
[49] *mistake*] take in error.
[50] *Hecate's ban*] the curse of Hecate, goddess of magic and the underworld.
[51] *usurp*] encroach.

HAM. What, frighted with false fire?[52]
QUEEN. How fares my lord?
POL. Give o'er the play.
KING. Give me some light. Away!
POL. Lights, lights, lights! [*Exeunt all but* HAMLET *and* HORATIO.
HAM.
Why, let the stricken deer go weep,
The hart ungalled play;
For some must watch, while some must sleep,
Thus runs the world away.

Would not this, sir, and a forest of feathers—if the rest of my fortunes turn Turk with me—with two Provincial roses[53] on my razed[54] shoes, get me a fellowship in a cry[55] of players, sir?

HOR. Half a share.
HAM. A whole one, I.

For thou dost know, O Damon dear,
This realm dismantled was
Of Jove himself; and now reigns here
A very, very—pajock.[56]

HOR. You might have rhymed.
HAM. O good Horatio, I'll take the ghost's word for a thousand pound. Didst perceive?
HOR. Very well, my lord.
HAM. Upon the talk of the poisoning?
HOR. I did very well note him.
HAM. Ah, ha! Come, some music; come, the recorders.

For if the King like not the comedy,
Why then, belike, he likes it not, perdy.[57]

Come, some music.

Enter ROSENCRANTZ *and* GUILDENSTERN.

GUIL. Good my lord, vouchsafe me a word with you.
HAM. Sir, a whole history.

[52] *false fire*] discharge of blank shots.
[53] *Provincial roses*] roses from Provins or from Provence.
[54] *razed*] slashed (in patterns). The feathers and decorated shoes were regularly part of an actor's costume.
[55] *cry*] pack.
[56] *pajock*] (?) peacock.
[57] *perdy*] a colloquial form of *pardieu*.

GUIL. The King, sir—

HAM. Ay, sir, what of him?

GUIL. Is in his retirement marvellous distempered.

HAM. With drink, sir?

GUIL. No, my lord, rather with choler.

HAM. Your wisdom should show itself more richer to signify this to the doctor; for, for me to put him to his purgation would perhaps plunge him into far more choler.

GUIL. Good my lord, put your discourse into some frame, and start not so wildly from my affair.

HAM. I am tame, sir. Pronounce.

GUIL. The Queen, your mother, in most great affliction of spirit, hath sent me to you.

HAM. You are welcome.

GUIL. Nay, good my lord, this courtesy is not of the right breed. If it shall please you to make me a wholesome answer, I will do your mother's commandment; if not, your pardon and my return shall be the end of my business.

HAM. Sir, I cannot.

GUIL. What, my lord?

HAM. Make you a wholesome answer. My wit's diseased. But, sir, such answer as I can make, you shall command, or rather, as you say, my mother. Therefore no more, but to the matter. My mother, you say—

ROS. Then thus she says: your behaviour hath struck her into amazement and admiration.[58]

HAM. O wonderful son, that can so astonish a mother! But is there no sequel at the heels of this mother's admiration? Impart.

ROS. She desires to speak with you in her closet, ere you go to bed.

HAM. We shall obey, were she ten times our mother. Have you any further trade with us?

ROS. My lord, you once did love me.

HAM. So I do still, by these pickers and stealers.[59]

ROS. Good my lord, what is your cause of distemper? You do surely bar the door upon your own liberty if you deny your griefs to your friend.

HAM. Sir, I lack advancement.

ROS. How can that be, when you have the voice of the King himself for your succession in Denmark?

[58] *admiration*] astonishment.

[59] *pickers and stealers*] i.e., hands.

HAM. Ay, sir, but 'while the grass grows'—the proverb is something musty.

Enter Players *with recorders.*

O, the recorders! Let me see one. To withdraw[60] with you:—why do you go about to recover the wind of[61] me, as if you would drive me into a toil?[62]

GUIL. O, my lord, if my duty be too bold, my love is too unmannerly.

HAM. I do not well understand that. Will you play upon this pipe?

GUIL. My lord, I cannot.

HAM. I pray you.

GUIL. Believe me, I cannot.

HAM. I do beseech you.

GUIL. I know no touch of it, my lord.

HAM. It is as easy as lying. Govern these ventages with your fingers and thumb, give it breath with your mouth, and it will discourse most eloquent music. Look you, these are the stops.

GUIL. But these cannot I command to any utterance of harmony. I have not the skill.

HAM. Why, look you now, how unworthy a thing you make of me. You would play upon me, you would seem to know my stops, you would pluck out the heart of my mystery, you would sound me from my lowest note to the top of my compass; and there is much music, excellent voice, in this little organ; yet cannot you make it speak. 'Sblood, do you think I am easier to be played on than a pipe? Call me what instrument you will, though you can fret me, yet you cannot play upon me.

Enter POLONIUS.

God bless you, sir.

POL. My lord, the Queen would speak with you, and presently.[63]

HAM. Do you see yonder cloud that's almost in shape of a camel?

POL. By the mass, and 'tis like a camel, indeed.

HAM. Methinks it is like a weasel.

POL. It is backed like a weasel.

HAM. Or like a whale?

[60] *withdraw*] i.e., to speak a word in private.

[61] *recover the wind of*] a hunting metaphor meaning "to get upwind of."

[62] *toil*] net.

[63] *presently*] immediately.

POL. Very like a whale.
HAM. Then I will come to my mother by and by. [*Aside*] They fool me to the top of my bent.[64]—I will come by and by.
POL. I will say so. [*Exit* POLONIUS.
HAM. 'By and by' is easily said. Leave me, friends.
[*Exeunt all but* HAMLET.
'Tis now the very witching time of night,
When churchyards yawn, and hell itself breathes out
Contagion to this world. Now could I drink hot blood,
And do such bitter business as the day
Would quake to look on. Soft, now to my mother.
O heart, lose not thy nature. Let not ever
The soul of Nero[65] enter this firm bosom.
Let me be cruel, not unnatural.
I will speak daggers to her, but use none.
My tongue and soul in this be hypocrites;
How in my words soever she be shent,[66]
To give them seals never my soul consent. [*Exit*.

SCENE III. *A room in the castle.*

Enter KING, ROSENCRANTZ, *and* GUILDENSTERN.

KING. I like him not, nor stands it safe with us
To let his madness range. Therefore prepare you.
I your commission will forthwith dispatch,
And he to England shall along with you.
The terms of our estate may not endure
Hazard so near us as doth hourly grow
Out of his brows.
GUIL. We will ourselves provide.[1]
Most holy and religious fear it is
To keep those many many bodies safe

[64] *the top of my bent*] to the utmost limit.
[65] *Nero*] the Roman emperor who put his mother, Agrippina, to death.
[66] *shent*] reproached.

[1] *provide*] equip.

That live and feed upon your Majesty.
ROS. The single and peculiar[2] life is bound
With all the strength and armour of the mind
To keep itself from noyance,[3] but much more
That spirit upon whose weal depends and rests
The lives of many. The cess[4] of majesty
Dies not alone, but like a gulf[5] doth draw
What's near it with it. It is a massy wheel,
Fix'd on the summit of the highest mount,
To whose huge spokes ten thousand lesser things
Are mortised and adjoin'd; which, when it falls,
Each small annexment, petty consequence,
Attends the boisterous ruin. Never alone
Did the King sigh, but with a general groan.
KING. Arm you,[6] I pray you, to this speedy voyage,
For we will fetters put about this fear,
Which now goes too free-footed.
ROS. }
GUIL. } We will haste us.

[*Exeunt* ROSENCRANTZ *and* GUILDENSTERN.

Enter POLONIUS.

POL. My lord, he's going to his mother's closet.
Behind the arras I'll convey myself,
To hear the process.[7] I'll warrant she'll tax him home.
And, as you said, and wisely was it said,
'Tis meet that some more audience than a mother,
Since nature makes them partial, should o'erhear
The speech, of vantage.[8] Fare you well, my liege.
I'll call upon you ere you go to bed,
And tell you what I know.
KING. Thanks, dear my lord.

[*Exit* POLONIUS.

O, my offence is rank, it smells to heaven.
It hath the primal eldest curse upon't,
A brother's murder. Pray can I not,

[2] *peculiar*] particular, individual.
[3] *noyance*] harm.
[4] *cess*] decease.
[5] *gulf*] whirlpool.
[6] *Arm you*] prepare, equip yourselves.
[7] *process*] proceedings.
[8] *of vantage*] besides.

Though inclination be as sharp as will;
My stronger guilt defeats my strong intent,
And, like a man to double business bound,
I stand in pause where I shall first begin,
And both neglect. What if this cursed hand
Were thicker than itself with brother's blood,
Is there not rain enough in the sweet heavens
To wash it white as snow? Whereto serves mercy
But to confront the visage of offence?
And what's in prayer but this twofold force,
To be forestalled ere we come to fall,
Or pardon'd being down? Then I'll look up.
My fault is past. But O, what form of prayer
Can serve my turn? 'Forgive me my foul murder?'
That cannot be, since I am still possess'd
Of those effects for which I did the murder—
My crown, mine own ambition and my queen.
May one be pardon'd and retain the offence?[9]
In the corrupted currents of this world
Offence's gilded hand may shove by justice,
And oft 'tis seen the wicked prize itself
Buys out the law. But 'tis not so above:
There is no shuffling,[10] there the action lies
In his true nature, and we ourselves compell'd
Even to the teeth and forehead of[11] our faults
To give in evidence. What then? What rests?
Try what repentance can. What can it not?
Yet what can it when one can not repent?
O wretched state, O bosom black as death,
O limed soul, that struggling to be free
Art more engaged! Help, angels! Make assay.
Bow, stubborn knees, and, heart with strings of steel,
Be soft as sinews of the new-born babe.
All may be well. [*Retires and kneels.*

Enter HAMLET.

HAM. Now might I do it pat, now he is praying.
And now I'll do't. And so he goes to heaven;

[9] *offence*] the fruits of the crime.
[10] *shuffling*] trickery.
[11] *to the teeth and forehead of*] face to face with.

And so am I revenged. That would be scann'd:[12]
A villain kills my father, and for that,
I, his sole son, do this same villain send
To heaven.
O, this is hire and salary, not revenge.
He took my father grossly, full of bread,
With all his crimes broad blown,[13] as flush[14] as May;
And how his audit stands who knows save heaven?
But in our circumstance[15] and course of thought,
'Tis heavy with him. And am I then revenged,
To take him in the purging of his soul,
When he is fit and season'd for his passage?
No.
Up, sword, and know thou a more horrid hent.[16]
When he is drunk asleep, or in his rage,
Or in the incestuous pleasure of his bed,
At game, a-swearing, or about some act
That has no relish of salvation in't,
Then trip him, that his heels may kick at heaven
And that his soul may be as damn'd and black
As hell, whereto it goes. My mother stays.
This physic[17] but prolongs thy sickly days. [*Exit.*

KING. [*Rising*] My words fly up, my thoughts remain below.
Words without thoughts never to heaven go. [*Exit.*

[12] *would be scann'd*] needs to be examined.
[13] *broad blown*] in full bloom.
[14] *flush*] lusty, in its prime.
[15] *in our circumstance*] viewed from our earthly perspective.
[16] *hent*] seizing, opportunity for seizing.
[17] *physic*] i.e., praying.

SCENE IV. *The Queen's closet.*

Enter QUEEN *and* POLONIUS.

POL. He will come straight. Look you lay home to him.[1]
Tell him his pranks have been too broad[2] to bear with,
And that your grace hath screen'd and stood between
Much heat and him. I'll silence me even here.
Pray you, be round[3] with him.

QUEEN. I'll warrant you,
Fear me not. Withdraw, I hear him coming.
[POLONIUS *hides behind the arras.*

Enter HAMLET.

HAM. Now, mother, what's the matter?

QUEEN. Hamlet, thou hast thy father much offended.

HAM. Mother, you have my father much offended.

QUEEN. Come, come, you answer with an idle tongue.

HAM. Go, go, you question with a wicked tongue.

QUEEN. Why, how now, Hamlet?

HAM. What's the matter now?

QUEEN. Have you forgot me?

HAM. No, by the rood, not so.
You are the Queen, your husband's brother's wife,
And—would it were not so—you are my mother.

QUEEN. Nay, then, I'll set those to you that can speak.

HAM. Come, come, and sit you down; you shall not budge.
You go not till I set you up a glass
Where you may see the inmost part of you.

QUEEN. What wilt thou do? Thou wilt not murder me?
Help, help, ho!

POL. [*Behind*] What, ho! Help, help, help!

HAM. [*Drawing*] How now, a rat? Dead for a ducat, dead.
[*Makes a pass through the arras.*

POL. [*Behind*] O, I am slain! [*Falls and dies.*

QUEEN. O me, what hast thou done?

[1] *lay home to him*] speak bluntly with him.
[2] *broad*] unrestrained.
[3] *round*] plain-spoken.

HAM. Nay, I know not. Is it the King?
QUEEN. O, what a rash and bloody deed is this!
HAM. A bloody deed. Almost as bad, good mother,
As kill a king and marry with his brother.
QUEEN. As kill a king?
HAM. Ay, lady, 'twas my word.
[*Lifts up the arras and discovers* POLONIUS.
Thou wretched, rash, intruding fool, farewell.
I took thee for thy better. Take thy fortune.
Thou find'st to be too busy is some danger.—
Leave wringing of your hands. Peace, sit you down,
And let me wring your heart; for so I shall,
If it be made of penetrable stuff,
If damned custom have not braz'd[4] it so,
That it be proof[5] and bulwark against sense.[6]
QUEEN. What have I done, that thou darest wag thy tongue
In noise so rude against me?
HAM. Such an act
That blurs the grace and blush of modesty,
Calls virtue hypocrite, takes off the rose
From the fair forehead of an innocent love,
And sets a blister[7] there, makes marriage vows
As false as dicers' oaths—O, such a deed
As from the body of contraction[8] plucks
The very soul, and sweet religion makes
A rhapsody[9] of words. Heaven's face doth glow,
Yea, this solidity and compound mass
With tristful visage, as against the doom,[10]
Is thought-sick at the act.
QUEEN. Ay me, what act,
That roars so loud and thunders in the index?[11]
HAM. Look here upon this picture, and on this,
The counterfeit presentment[12] of two brothers.
See what a grace was seated on this brow:

[4] *braz'd*] coated with brass, hardened.
[5] *proof*] impenetrable.
[6] *sense*] reason.
[7] *blister*] prostitutes were branded on the forehead.
[8] *contraction*] the marriage contract.
[9] *rhapsody*] cento, amalgam of empty words.
[10] *against the doom*] in expectation of the Judgment Day.
[11] *index*] preface, prologue.
[12] *counterfeit presentment*] representation, portrait.

Hyperion's curls, the front[13] of Jove himself,
An eye like Mars, to threaten and command,
A station[14] like the herald Mercury
New-lighted on a heaven-kissing hill,
A combination and a form indeed
Where every god did seem to set his seal
To give the world assurance of a man.
This was your husband. Look you now, what follows.
Here is your husband: like a mildew'd ear,
Blasting[15] his wholesome brother. Have you eyes?
Could you on this fair mountain leave[16] to feed,
And batten on this moor? Ha, have you eyes?
You cannot call it love, for at your age
The heyday in the blood is tame, it's humble,
And waits upon the judgement; and what judgement
Would step from this to this? Sense[17] sure you have,
Else could you not have motion, but sure that sense
Is apoplex'd, for madness would not err,
Nor sense to ecstasy[18] was ne'er so thrall'd
But it reserved some quantity of choice,
To serve in such a difference. What devil was't
That thus hath cozen'd you at hoodman-blind?[19]
Eyes without feeling, feeling without sight,
Ears without hands or eyes, smelling sans all,
Or but a sickly part of one true sense
Could not so mope.[20]
O shame, where is thy blush? Rebellious hell,
If thou canst mutine in a matron's bones,
To flaming youth let virtue be as wax
And melt in her own fire. Proclaim no shame
When the compulsive ardour gives the charge,[21]
Since frost itself as actively doth burn,
And reason panders will.

QUEEN. O Hamlet, speak no more.

[13] *front*] forehead.
[14] *station*] stance.
[15] *Blasting*] blighting, causing to wither.
[16] *leave*] cease.
[17] *Sense*] the faculties and act of perception.
[18] *ecstasy*] delusion, madness.
[19] *hoodman-blind*] blindman's buff.
[20] *mope*] act without thought.
[21] *gives the charge*] attacks.

Thou turn'st mine eyes into my very soul,
And there I see such black and grained[22] spots
As will not leave their tinct.

HAM. Nay, but to live
In the rank sweat of an enseamed[23] bed,
Stew'd in corruption, honeying and making love
Over the nasty sty—

QUEEN. O, speak to me no more.
These words like daggers enter in my ears.
No more, sweet Hamlet.

HAM. A murderer and a villain,
A slave that is not twentieth part the tithe
Of your precedent lord, a vice[24] of kings,
A cutpurse of the empire and the rule,
That from a shelf the precious diadem stole
And put it in his pocket—

QUEEN. No more.

HAM. A king of shreds and patches—

Enter GHOST.

Save me, and hover o'er me with your wings,
You heavenly guards! What would your gracious figure?

QUEEN. Alas, he's mad.

HAM. Do you not come your tardy son to chide,
That, lapsed in time and passion, lets go by
The important[25] acting of your dread command?
O, say!

GHOST. Do not forget. This visitation
Is but to whet thy almost blunted purpose.
But look, amazement on thy mother sits.
O, step between her and her fighting soul.
Conceit[26] in weakest bodies strongest works.
Speak to her, Hamlet.

HAM. How is it with you, lady?

QUEEN. Alas, how is't with you,
That you do bend your eye on vacancy
And with the incorporal air do hold discourse?

[22] *grained*] dyed in grain, which was a red dye made from the dried bodies of insects.
[23] *enseamed*] filthy.
[24] *vice*] the buffoon-like character of Morality plays.
[25] *important*] urgent.
[26] *Conceit*] imagination.

Forth at your eyes your spirits wildly peep,
And, as the sleeping soldiers in the alarm,[27]
Your bedded hair, like life in excrements,[28]
Start up and stand an end. O gentle son,
Upon the heat and flame of thy distemper
Sprinkle cool patience. Whereon do you look?

HAM. On him, on him. Look you how pale he glares.
His form and cause conjoin'd, preaching to stones,
Would make them capable.[29]—Do not look upon me,
Lest with this piteous action you convert
My stern effects.[30] Then what I have to do
Will want true colour—tears perchance for blood.

QUEEN. To whom do you speak this?

HAM. Do you see nothing there?

QUEEN. Nothing at all; yet all that is I see.

HAM. Nor did you nothing hear?

QUEEN. No, nothing but ourselves.

HAM. Why, look you there. Look how it steals away.
My father, in his habit[31] as he lived.
Look where he goes, even now, out at the portal. [*Exit* GHOST.

QUEEN. This is the very coinage of your brain.
This bodily creation ecstasy[32]
Is very cunning in.

HAM. Ecstasy?
My pulse, as yours, doth temperately keep time,
And makes as healthful music. It is not madness
That I have utter'd. Bring me to the test,
And I the matter will re-word, which madness
Would gambol[33] from. Mother, for love of grace,
Lay not that flattering unction[34] to your soul,
That not your trespass but my madness speaks.
It will but skin[35] and film the ulcerous place,
Whiles rank corruption, mining all within,
Infects unseen. Confess yourself to heaven,
Repent what's past, avoid what is to come,

[27] *in the alarm*] at the call to arms.
[28] *excrements*] growths out from the body.
[29] *capable*] responsive.
[30] *effects*] intended actions.
[31] *his habit*] appearance.
[32] *ecstasy*] madness.
[33] *gambol*] skip, shy away.
[34] *unction*] salve, ointment.
[35] *skin*] cover with skin.

And do not spread the compost on the weeds,
To make them ranker. Forgive me this my virtue,
For in the fatness of these pursy[36] times
Virtue itself of vice must pardon beg,
Yea, curb[37] and woo for leave to do him good.

QUEEN. O Hamlet, thou hast cleft my heart in twain.

HAM. O, throw away the worser part of it
And live the purer with the other half.
Good night. But go not to my uncle's bed.
Assume[38] a virtue, if you have it not.
That monster, custom, who all sense doth eat,
Of habits evil, is angel yet in this,
That to the use of actions fair and good
He likewise gives a frock or livery,
That aptly is put on. Refrain tonight
And that shall lend a kind of easiness
To the next abstinence, the next more easy;
For use almost can change the stamp of nature
And either master the devil, or throw him out
With wondrous potency. Once more, good night;
And when you are desirous to be blest,
I'll blessing beg of you. For this same lord, [*Pointing to* POLONIUS.
I do repent. But heaven hath pleased it so,
To punish me with this, and this with me,
That I must be their scourge and minister.
I will bestow[39] him, and will answer well
The death I gave him. So, again, good night.
I must be cruel, only to be kind.
This bad begins, and worse remains behind.[40]
One word more, good lady.

QUEEN. What shall I do?

HAM. Not this, by no means, that I bid you do:
Let the bloat King tempt you again to bed,
Pinch wanton on your cheek, call you his mouse,
And let him, for a pair of reechy[41] kisses,
Or paddling[42] in your neck with his damn'd fingers,
Make you to ravel all this matter out,

[36] *pursy*] flabby.
[37] *curb*] bow.
[38] *Assume*] take on, adopt.
[39] *bestow*] dispose of.
[40] *behind*] i.e., to come.
[41] *reechy*] filthy, stinking.
[42] *paddling*] playing amorously.

That I essentially am not in madness,
But mad in craft. 'Twere good you let him know;
For who, that's but a queen, fair, sober, wise,
Would from a paddock,[43] from a bat, a gib,[44]
Such dear concernings hide? Who would do so?
No, in despite of sense and secrecy,
Unpeg the basket on the house's top,
Let the birds fly, and like the famous ape,[45]
To try conclusions, in the basket creep
And break your own neck down.

QUEEN. Be thou assured, if words be made of breath
And breath of life, I have no life to breathe
What thou hast said to me.

HAM. I must to England; you know that?

QUEEN. Alack,
I had forgot. 'Tis so concluded on.

HAM. There's letters seal'd, and my two schoolfellows,
Whom I will trust as I will adders fang'd,
They bear the mandate. They must sweep my way,
And marshal me to knavery.[46] Let it work;
For 'tis the sport to have the enginer[47]
Hoist[48] with his own petard;[49] and't shall go hard
But I will delve one yard below their mines,
And blow them at the moon. O, 'tis most sweet
When in one line[50] two crafts[51] directly meet.
This man shall set me packing.[52]
I'll lug the guts into the neighbour room.
Mother, good night indeed. This counsellor
Is now most still, most secret and most grave,
Who was in life a foolish prating knave.
Come, sir, to draw toward an end with you.
Good night, mother.

[*Exeunt severally;* HAMLET *dragging in* POLONIUS.

[43] *paddock*] toad.
[44] *gib*] tomcat.
[45] *famous ape*] the ape, seeing the birds flying, imitates them and ends badly.
[46] *marshal me to knavery*] lead me to suffer knavery.
[47] *enginer*] creator of military hardware.
[48] *Hoist*] blown up.
[49] *petard*] explosive device.
[50] *in one line*] head on.
[51] *crafts*] plots.
[52] *packing*] (1) off in a hurry; (2) plotting.

ACT IV.

SCENE I. *A room in the castle.*

Enter KING, QUEEN, ROSENCRANTZ, *and* GUILDENSTERN.

KING. There's matter in these sighs, these profound heaves;
You must translate. 'Tis fit we understand them.
Where is your son?

QUEEN. Bestow this place on us a little while.
[*Exeunt* ROSENCRANTZ *and* GUILDENSTERN.
Ah, mine own lord, what have I seen tonight!

KING. What, Gertrude? How does Hamlet?

QUEEN. Mad as the sea and wind, when both contend
Which is the mightier. In his lawless fit,
Behind the arras hearing something stir,
Whips out his rapier, cries 'A rat, a rat!'
And in this brainish[1] apprehension kills
The unseen good old man.

KING. O heavy deed!
It had been so with us, had we been there.
His liberty is full of threats to all,
To you yourself, to us, to everyone.
Alas, how shall this bloody deed be answer'd?
It will be laid to us, whose providence
Should have kept short,[2] restrain'd and out of haunt,[3]
This mad young man. But so much was our love,
We would not understand what was most fit,
But, like the owner of a foul disease,
To keep it from divulging,[4] let it feed

[1] *brainish*] brainsick.
[2] *short*] i.e., on a short leash.
[3] *out of haunt*] away from any public place.
[4] *divulging*] becoming known.

Even on the pith of life. Where is he gone?

QUEEN. To draw apart the body he hath kill'd,
O'er whom—his very madness, like some ore[5]
Among a mineral[6] of metals base,
Shows itself pure—he weeps for what is done.

KING. O Gertrude, come away.
The sun no sooner shall the mountains touch,
But we will ship him hence; and this vile deed
We must, with all our majesty and skill,
Both countenance and excuse. Ho, Guildenstern!

Enter ROSENCRANTZ *and* GUILDENSTERN.

Friends both, go join you with some further aid.
Hamlet in madness hath Polonius slain,
And from his mother's closet hath he dragg'd him.
Go seek him out, speak fair, and bring the body
Into the chapel. I pray you, haste in this.
[*Exeunt* ROSENCRANTZ *and* GUILDENSTERN.
Come, Gertrude, we'll call up our wisest friends,
And let them know, both what we mean to do,
And what's untimely done. So . . . slander,[7]
Whose whisper o'er the world's diameter
As level[8] as the cannon to his blank[9]
Transports his poison'd shot, may miss our name
And hit the woundless[10] air. O, come away.
My soul is full of discord and dismay. [*Exeunt*.

[5] *ore*] precious metal, perhaps gold.
[6] *mineral*] mine.
[7] *So . . . slander*] a defective line.
[8] *level*] straight.
[9] *blank*] target.
[10] *woundless*] invulnerable.

SCENE II. *Another room in the castle.*

Enter HAMLET.

HAM. Safely stowed.

ROS. / GUIL. [*Within*] Hamlet! Lord Hamlet!

HAM. But soft, what noise? Who calls on Hamlet? O, here they come.

Enter ROSENCRANTZ *and* GUILDENSTERN.

ROS. What have you done, my lord, with the dead body?

HAM. Compounded it with dust, whereto 'tis kin.

ROS. Tell us where 'tis, that we may take it thence and bear it to the chapel.

HAM. Do not believe it.

ROS. Believe what?

HAM. That I can keep your counsel and not mine own. Besides, to be demanded of a sponge—what replication[1] should be made by the son of a king?

ROS. Take you me for a sponge, my lord?

HAM. Ay, sir, that soaks up the King's countenance,[2] his rewards, his authorities. But such officers do the King best service in the end. He keeps them, like an ape, in the corner of his jaw—first mouthed, to be last swallowed. When he needs what you have gleaned, it is but squeezing you, and, sponge, you shall be dry again.

ROS. I understand you not, my lord.

HAM. I am glad of it. A knavish speech sleeps in a foolish ear.

ROS. My lord, you must tell us where the body is, and go with us to the King.

HAM. The body is with the King, but the King is not with the body. The King is a thing—

GUIL. A thing, my lord?

HAM. Of nothing. Bring me to him. [*Exeunt.*

[1] *replication*] reply.

[2] *countenance*] patronage, favor.

SCENE III. *Another room in the castle.*

Enter KING, *attended.*

KING. I have sent to seek him, and to find the body.
How dangerous is it that this man goes loose!
Yet must not we put the strong law on him.
He's loved of the distracted[1] multitude,
Who like not in their judgement, but their eyes;
And where 'tis so, the offender's scourge[2] is weigh'd,
But never the offence. To bear all smooth and even,
This sudden sending him away must seem
Deliberate pause.[3] Diseases desperate grown
By desperate appliance[4] are relieved,
Or not at all.

Enter ROSENCRANTZ.

How now, what hath befall'n?
ROS. Where the dead body is bestow'd, my lord,
We cannot get from him.
KING. But where is he?
ROS. Without, my lord; guarded, to know your pleasure.
KING. Bring him before us.
ROS. Ho, Guildenstern! Bring in my lord.

Enter HAMLET *and* GUILDENSTERN.

KING. Now, Hamlet, where's Polonius?
HAM. At supper.
KING. At supper? Where?
HAM. Not where he eats, but where he is eaten. A certain convocation of politic worms are e'en at him. Your worm is your only emperor for diet. We fat all creatures else to fat us, and we fat ourselves for maggots. Your fat king and your lean beggar is but variable service,[5] two dishes, but to one table. That's the end.

[1] *distracted*] irrational, unthinking.
[2] *scourge*] punishment.
[3] *Deliberate pause*] the result of careful consideration.
[4] *appliance*] cure, treatment.
[5] *service*] course (of food).

KING. Alas, alas!

HAM. A man may fish with the worm that hath eat of a king, and eat of the fish that hath fed of that worm.

KING. What dost thou mean by this?

HAM. Nothing but to show you how a king may go a progress[6] through the guts of a beggar.

KING. Where is Polonius?

HAM. In heaven. Send thither to see. If your messenger find him not there, seek him i' the other place yourself. But indeed, if you find him not within this month, you shall nose him as you go up the stairs into the lobby.

KING. [*To some* Attendants] Go seek him there.

HAM. He will stay till you come. [*Exeunt* Attendants.

KING. Hamlet, this deed, for thine especial safety—
Which we do tender,[7] as we dearly grieve
For that which thou hast done—must send thee hence
With fiery quickness. Therefore prepare thyself.
The bark is ready and the wind at help,[8]
The associates tend,[9] and everything is bent
For England.

HAM. For England?

KING. Ay, Hamlet.

HAM. Good.

KING. So is it, if thou knew'st our purposes.

HAM. I see a cherub that sees them. But, come; for England. Farewell, dear mother.

KING. Thy loving father, Hamlet.

HAM. My mother. Father and mother is man and wife, man and wife is one flesh, and so, my mother. Come, for England. [*Exit.*

KING. Follow him at foot.[10] Tempt him with speed aboard.
Delay it not. I'll have him hence tonight.
Away, for every thing is seal'd and done
That else leans on the affair. Pray you, make haste.
[*Exeunt* ROSENCRANTZ *and* GUILDENSTERN.
And, England,[11] if my love thou hold'st at aught—
As my great power thereof may give thee sense,
Since yet thy cicatrice looks raw and red

[6] *progress*] journey made by a sovereign.
[7] *tender*] hold dear.
[8] *at help*] favorable.
[9] *tend*] attend, are in waiting.
[10] *at foot*] closely.
[11] *England*] the King of England.

After the Danish sword, and thy free awe
Pays homage to us—thou mayst not coldly set[12]
Our sovereign process;[13] which imports at full,
By letters congruing to[14] that effect,
The present[15] death of Hamlet. Do it, England;
For like the hectic[16] in my blood he rages,
And thou must cure me. Till I know 'tis done,
Howe'er my haps, my joys were ne'er begun. [*Exit.*

SCENE IV. *A plain in Denmark.*

Enter FORTINBRAS, *a* Captain *and* Soldiers, *marching.*

FOR. Go, captain, from me greet the Danish king.
Tell him that by his license Fortinbras
Craves the conveyance of a promised march
Over his kingdom. You know the rendezvous.
If that his Majesty would aught with us,
We shall express our duty in his eye;[1]
And let him know so.

CAP. I will do't, my lord.

FOR. Go softly on. [*Exeunt* FORTINBRAS *and* Soldiers.

Enter HAMLET, ROSENCRANTZ, GUILDENSTERN, *and others.*

HAM. Good sir, whose powers are these?

CAP. They are of Norway, sir.

HAM. How purposed, sir, I pray you?

CAP. Against some part of Poland.

HAM. Who commands them, sir?

CAP. The nephew to old Norway, Fortinbras.

HAM. Goes it against the main of Poland, sir,
Or for some frontier?

[12] *coldly set*] regard with indifference.
[13] *process*] mandate.
[14] *congruing to*] in accordance with.
[15] *present*] immediate.
[16] *hectic*] fever.

---

[1] *express . . . eye*] pay our respects to him in person.

CAP. Truly to speak, and with no addition,
We go to gain a little patch of ground
That hath in it no profit but the name.
To pay five ducats, five, I would not farm[2] it,
Nor will it yield to Norway or the Pole
A ranker[3] rate, should it be sold in fee.[4]
HAM. Why, then the Polack never will defend it.
CAP. Yes, it is already garrison'd.
HAM. Two thousand souls and twenty thousand ducats
Will not debate the question of this straw!
This is the imposthume[5] of much wealth and peace,
That inward breaks, and shows no cause without
Why the man dies. I humbly thank you, sir.
CAP. God be wi' you, sir. [*Exit*.
ROS. Will't please you go, my lord?
HAM. I'll be with you straight. Go a little before.
[*Exeunt all but* HAMLET.
How all occasions do inform against me,
And spur my dull revenge. What is a man,
If his chief good and market of his time
Be but to sleep and feed? A beast, no more.
Sure, he that made us with such large discourse,[6]
Looking before and after, gave us not
That capability and godlike reason
To fust[7] in us unused. Now, whether it be
Bestial oblivion, or some craven scruple
Of thinking too precisely on the event—
A thought which, quarter'd, hath but one part wisdom
And ever three parts coward—I do not know
Why yet I live to say this thing's to do,
Sith I have cause, and will, and strength, and means,
To do't. Examples gross as earth exhort me:
Witness this army, of such mass and charge,[8]
Led by a delicate and tender prince,
Whose spirit with divine ambition puff'd
Makes mouths at the invisible event,

[2] *farm*] take the lease of.
[3] *ranker*] greater.
[4] *in fee*] outright, freehold.
[5] *imposthume*] abscess.
[6] *discourse*] faculty of reason.
[7] *fust*] grow moldy.
[8] *charge*] expense, cost.

Exposing what is mortal and unsure
To all that fortune, death and danger dare,
Even for an eggshell. Rightly to be great
Is not to stir without great argument,
But greatly to find quarrel in a straw
When honour's at the stake. How stand I then,
That have a father kill'd, a mother stain'd,
Excitements of my reason and my blood,
And let all sleep, while to my shame I see
The imminent death of twenty thousand men,
That for a fantasy and trick[9] of fame
Go to their graves like beds, fight for a plot
Whereon the numbers cannot try the cause,[10]
Which is not tomb enough and continent
To hide the slain? O, from this time forth,
My thoughts be bloody, or be nothing worth. [*Exit.*

SCENE V. *Elsinore. A room in the castle.*

Enter QUEEN, HORATIO, *and a* Gentleman.

QUEEN. I will not speak with her.
GENT. She is importunate,
Indeed distract.[1] Her mood will needs be pitied.
QUEEN. What would she have?
GENT. She speaks much of her father, says she hears
There's tricks i' the world, and hems and beats her heart,
Spurns enviously[2] at straws, speaks things in doubt,[3]
That carry but half sense. Her speech is nothing,
Yet the unshaped use of it doth move
The hearers to collection.[4] They aim at it,
And botch the words up fit to their own thoughts,
Which, as her winks and nods and gestures yield them,

[9] *trick*] trifle.
[10] *Whereon . . . cause*] i.e., the disputed territory is not large enough to be the battlefield.

---

[1] *distract*] mad.
[2] *enviously*] spitefully.
[3] *in doubt*] ambiguously.
[4] *collection*] make inferences.

Indeed would make one think there might be thought,
Though nothing sure, yet much unhappily.[5]

HOR. 'Twere good she were spoken with, for she may strew
Dangerous conjectures in ill-breeding minds.

QUEEN. Let her come in. [*Exit* Gentleman.
[*Aside*] To my sick soul, as sin's true nature is,
Each toy[6] seems prologue to some great amiss.[7]
So full of artless jealousy[8] is guilt,
It spills[9] itself in fearing to be spilt.

Enter Gentleman, *with* OPHELIA.

OPH. Where is the beauteous Majesty of Denmark?

QUEEN. How now, Ophelia?

OPH. [*Sings*] How should I your true love know
From another one?
By his cockle hat and staff
And his sandal shoon.[10]

QUEEN. Alas, sweet lady, what imports this song?

OPH. Say you? Nay, pray you, mark.

[*Sings*] He is dead and gone, lady,
He is dead and gone;
At his head a grass-green turf,
At his heels a stone.

Oh, oh!

QUEEN. Nay, but, Ophelia—

OPH. Pray you, mark.

[*Sings*] White his shroud as the mountain snow—

Enter KING.

QUEEN. Alas, look here, my lord.

OPH. [*Sings*] Larded[11] with sweet flowers,
Which bewept to the grave did go
With true-love showers.

[5] *unhappily*] mischievously.
[6] *toy*] trifle.
[7] *great amiss*] calamity.
[8] *jealousy*] apprehension.
[9] *spills*] destroys.
[10] *cockle hat . . . shoon*] The lover is dressed as a pilgrim. *Shoon* is the archaic plural of "shoe."
[11] *Larded*] garnished, adorned.

KING. How do you, pretty lady?

OPH. Well, God 'ild you.[12] They say the owl was a baker's daughter. Lord, we know what we are, but know not what we may be. God be at your table.

KING. Conceit upon her father.

OPH. Pray you, let's have no words of this; but when they ask you what it means, say you this:

[*Sings*] Tomorrow is Saint Valentine's day,
All in the morning betime,
And I a maid at your window,
To be your Valentine.

Then up he rose, and donn'd his clothes,
And dupp'd[13] the chamber door,
Let in the maid, that out a maid
Never departed more.

KING. Pretty Ophelia—

OPH. Indeed, without an oath, I'll make an end on't.

[*Sings*] By Gis[14] and by Saint Charity,
Alack, and fie for shame!
Young men will do't, if they come to't,
By Cock,[15] they are to blame.

Quoth she, 'Before you tumbled me,
You promised me to wed.'

He answers:

'So would I ha' done, by yonder sun,
An thou hadst not come to my bed.'

KING. How long hath she been thus?

OPH. I hope all will be well. We must be patient. But I cannot choose but weep, to think they should lay him i' the cold ground. My brother shall know of it. And so I thank you for your good counsel. Come, my coach. Good night, ladies; good night, sweet ladies; good night, good night. [*Exit.*

KING. Follow her close. Give her good watch, I pray you.
[*Exit* HORATIO.
O, this is the poison of deep grief; it springs

[12] *God 'ild you*] God yield (reward) you.
[13] *dupp'd*] opened.
[14] *Gis*] a corruption of "Jesus."
[15] *Cock*] a corruption of "God."

All from her father's death. O Gertrude, Gertrude,
When sorrows come, they come not single spies,[16]
But in battalions. First, her father slain;
Next, your son gone, and he most violent author
Of his own just remove; the people muddied,
Thick and unwholesome in their thoughts and whispers,
For good Polonius' death; and we have done but greenly,[17]
In hugger-mugger[18] to inter him; poor Ophelia
Divided from herself and her fair judgement,
Without the which we are pictures, or mere beasts;
Last, and as much containing as all these,
Her brother is in secret come from France,
Feeds on his wonder,[19] keeps himself in clouds,
And wants not buzzers[20] to infect his ear
With pestilent speeches of his father's death;
Wherein necessity, of matter beggar'd,
Will nothing stick[21] our person to arraign[22]
In ear and ear. O my dear Gertrude, this,
Like to a murdering-piece,[23] in many places
Gives me superfluous death. [*A noise within.*

QUEEN. Alack, what noise is this?

KING. Where are my Switzers?[24] Let them guard the door.

Enter another Gentleman.

What is the matter?

GENT. Save yourself, my lord.
The ocean, overpeering of his list,[25]
Eats not the flats with more impetuous haste
Than young Laertes, in a riotous head,[26]
O'erbears your officers. The rabble call him lord;
And, as the world were now but to begin,
Antiquity forgot, custom not known—

[16] *spies*] advance guards.
[17] *greenly*] foolishly.
[18] *In hugger-mugger*] clandestinely.
[19] *wonder*] bewilderment.
[20] *wants not buzzers*] does not lack rumor-mongers.
[21] *nothing stick*] not hesitate.
[22] *arraign*] accuse.
[23] *murdering-piece*] a type of cannon firing grapeshot.
[24] *Switzers*] Swiss mercenaries, used as a personal bodyguard.
[25] *overpeering of his list*] rising above its boundary.
[26] *head*] armed force.

The ratifiers and props of every word—
They cry 'Choose we! Laertes shall be king.'
Caps, hands and tongues applaud it to the clouds,
'Laertes shall be king, Laertes king.'

QUEEN. How cheerfully on the false trail they cry.[27]
O, this is counter, you false Danish dogs! [*Noise within.*

KING. The doors are broke.

Enter LAERTES, *armed;* Danes *following.*

LAER. Where is this King? Sirs, stand you all without.

DANES. No, let's come in.

LAER. I pray you, give me leave.

DANES. We will, we will.

LAER. I thank you. Keep the door. [*They retire without the door.*
O thou vile king,
Give me my father.

QUEEN. Calmly, good Laertes.

LAER. That drop of blood that's calm proclaims me bastard,
Cries cuckold to my father, brands the harlot
Even here, between the chaste unsmirched brows
Of my true mother.

KING. What is the cause, Laertes,
That thy rebellion looks so giant-like?
Let him go, Gertrude. Do not fear[28] our person.
There's such divinity doth hedge a king
That treason can but peep to what it would,
Acts little of his will. Tell me, Laertes,
Why thou art thus incensed. Let him go, Gertrude.
Speak, man.

LAER. Where is my father?

KING. Dead.

QUEEN. But not by him.

KING. Let him demand his fill.

LAER. How came he dead? I'll not be juggled with.
To hell, allegiance! Vows, to the blackest devil!
Conscience and grace, to the profoundest pit!
I dare damnation. To this point I stand,
That both the worlds I give to negligence,

[27] *cry*] make the sound of hounds.
[28] *fear*] fear for.

Let come what comes; only I'll be revenged
Most throughly[29] for my father.

KING. Who shall stay you?

LAER. My will, not all the world.
And for my means, I'll husband them so well,
They shall go far with little.

KING. Good Laertes,
If you desire to know the certainty
Of your dear father's death, is't writ in your revenge
That, swoopstake,[30] you will draw both friend and foe,
Winner and loser?

LAER. None but his enemies.

KING. Will you know them then?

LAER. To his good friends thus wide I'll ope my arms,
And, like the kind[31] life-rendering pelican,
Repast them with my blood.

KING. Why, now you speak
Like a good child and a true gentleman.
That I am guiltless of your father's death,
And am most sensibly[32] in grief for it,
It shall as level to your judgement pierce
As day does to your eye.

DANES. [*Within*] Let her come in.

LAER. How now, what noise is that?

Enter OPHELIA.

O heat, dry up my brains! Tears seven times salt,
Burn out the sense and virtue[33] of mine eye!
By heaven, thy madness shall be paid with weight,
Till our scale turn the beam. O rose of May!
Dear maid, kind sister, sweet Ophelia!
O heavens, is't possible a young maid's wits
Should be as mortal as an old man's life?
Nature is fine in love, and where 'tis fine
It sends some precious instance[34] of itself
After the thing it loves.

[29] *throughly*] thoroughly.
[30] *swoopstake*] sweepstake; i.e., indiscriminately.
[31] *kind*] behaving in accordance with its nature.
[32] *sensibly*] feelingly.
[33] *virtue*] power.
[34] *instance*] specimen, sample.

OPH. [*Sings*] They bore him barefaced on the bier;
And in his grave rain'd many a tear—

Fare you well, my dove.

LAER. Hadst thou thy wits, and didst persuade revenge,
It could not move thus.

OPH. You must sing 'down a-down,' and you 'Call him a-down-a.' O, how the wheel[35] becomes it! It is the false steward that stole his master's daughter.

LAER. This nothing's more than matter.

OPH. There's rosemary, that's for remembrance. Pray you, love, remember. And there is pansies, that's for thoughts.

LAER. A document in madness: thoughts and remembrance fitted.

OPH. There's fennel for you, and columbines.[36] There's rue for you, and here's some for me. We may call it herb of grace[37] o' Sundays. O, you must wear your rue with a difference.[38] There's a daisy.[39] I would give you some violets,[40] but they withered all when my father died. They say a made a good end—

[*Sings*] For bonny sweet Robin is all my joy.

LAER. Thought[41] and affliction, passion,[42] hell itself,
She turns to favour and to prettiness.

OPH. [*Sings*] And will a not come again?
And will a not come again?
No, no, he is dead,
Go to thy death-bed,
He never will come again.

His beard was as white as snow,
All flaxen was his poll.
He is gone, he is gone,
And we cast away moan.
God ha' mercy on his soul.

And of[43] all Christian souls, I pray God. God be wi' you.
[*Exit.*

[35] *wheel*] poetic refrain, burden.
[36] *fennel . . . columbines*] plants signifying infidelity.
[37] *rue . . . herb of grace*] plant signifying repentance.
[38] *a difference*] a mark of distinction, in heraldry.
[39] *daisy*] signifying unhappy love.
[40] *violets*] signifying faithfulness.
[41] *Thought*] sorrow, melancholy thought.
[42] *passion*] grief.
[43] *of*] on.

LAER. Do you see this, O God?

KING. Laertes, I must commune with your grief,
Or you deny me right. Go but apart,
Make choice of whom your wisest friends you will,
And they shall hear and judge 'twixt you and me.
If by direct or by collateral[44] hand
They find us touch'd,[45] we will our kingdom give,
Our crown, our life, and all that we call ours,
To you in satisfaction. But if not,
Be you content to lend your patience to us,
And we shall jointly labour with your soul
To give it due content.

LAER. Let this be so.
His means of death, his obscure funeral—
No trophy,[46] sword, nor hatchment[47] o'er his bones,
No noble rite nor formal ostentation—[48]
Cry to be heard, as 'twere from heaven to earth,
That I must call't in question.

KING. So you shall.
And where the offence is, let the great axe fall.
I pray you, go with me. [*Exeunt.*

SCENE VI. *Another room in the castle.*

Enter HORATIO *and a* Servant.

HOR. What are they that would speak with me?

SERV. Seafaring men, sir. They say they have letters for you.

HOR. Let them come in. [*Exit* Servant.
I do not know from what part of the world
I should be greeted, if not from Lord Hamlet.

Enter Sailors.

FIRST SAIL. God bless you, sir.

[44] *collateral*] indirect.
[45] *touch'd*] implicated.
[46] *trophy*] memorial.
[47] *hatchment*] armorial escutcheon.
[48] *ostentation*] ceremony.

HOR. Let him bless thee too.

FIRST SAIL. He shall, sir, an't please him. There's a letter for you, sir. It comes from the ambassador that was bound for England—if your name be Horatio, as I am let to know it is.

HOR. [*Reads*] Horatio, when thou shalt have overlooked[1] this, give these fellows some means to the King. They have letters for him. Ere we were two days old at sea, a pirate of very warlike appointment gave us chase. Finding ourselves too slow of sail, we put on a compelled valour, and in the grapple I boarded them. On the instant they got clear of our ship; so I alone became their prisoner. They have dealt with me like thieves of mercy; but they knew what they did: I am to do a turn for them. Let the King have the letters I have sent, and repair thou to me with as much speed as thou wouldest fly death. I have words to speak in thine ear will make thee dumb, yet are they much too light for the bore[2] of the matter. These good fellows will bring thee where I am. Rosencrantz and Guildenstern hold their course for England. Of them I have much to tell thee. Farewell.

He that thou knowest thine, HAMLET.

Come, I will make you way for these your letters,
And do't the speedier, that you may direct me
To him from whom you brought them. [*Exeunt.*

SCENE VII. *Another room in the castle.*

Enter KING *and* LAERTES.

KING. Now must your conscience my acquittance seal,
And you must put me in your heart for friend,
Sith you have heard, and with a knowing ear,
That he which hath your noble father slain
Pursued my life.

LAER. It well appears. But tell me
Why you proceeded not against these feats,[1]
So crimeful and so capital[2] in nature,

[1] *overlooked*] looked over, read.
[2] *too light for the bore*] i.e., Hamlet's words are like shot too light for the bore of the gun.

---

[1] *feats*] wicked deeds.
[2] *capital*] punishable by death.

As by your safety, wisdom, all things else,
You mainly[3] were stirr'd up.

KING. O, for two special reasons,
Which may to you perhaps seem much unsinew'd,
But yet to me they're strong. The Queen his mother
Lives almost by his looks; and for myself—
My virtue or my plague, be it either which—
She's so conjunctive[4] to my life and soul
That, as the star moves not but in his sphere,
I could not but by her. The other motive,
Why to a public count[5] I might not go,
Is the great love the general gender[6] bear him,
Who, dipping all his faults in their affection,
Would, like the spring that turneth wood to stone,
Convert his gyves[7] to graces; so that my arrows,
Too slightly timber'd for so loud a wind,
Would have reverted to my bow again
And not where I had aim'd them.

LAER. And so have I a noble father lost,
A sister driven into desperate terms,[8]
Whose worth, if praises may go back again,[9]
Stood challenger on mount of all the age
For her perfections. But my revenge will come.

KING. Break not your sleeps for that. You must not think
That we are made of stuff so flat and dull
That we can let our beard be shook with danger
And think it pastime. You shortly shall hear more.
I loved your father, and we love ourself.
And that, I hope, will teach you to imagine—

Enter a Messenger, *with letters.*

How now? What news?

MESS. Letters, my lord, from Hamlet.
This to your Majesty; this to the Queen.

KING. From Hamlet? Who brought them?

MESS. Sailors, my lord, they say. I saw them not.

[3] *mainly*] mightily.
[4] *conjunctive*] closely joined.
[5] *count*] reckoning, account.
[6] *general gender*] common people.
[7] *gyves*] chains, fetters; here, deficiencies.
[8] *terms*] circumstances.
[9] *go back again*] i.e., to what she was before she lapsed into madness.

They were given me by Claudio. He received them
Of him that brought them.

KING. Laertes, you shall hear them.—
Leave us. [*Exit* Messenger.

[*Reads*] High and mighty, you shall know I am set naked[10] on your kingdom. Tomorrow shall I beg leave to see your kingly eyes, when I shall, first asking your pardon, thereunto recount the occasion of my sudden and more strange return.

HAMLET.

What should this mean? Are all the rest come back?
Or is it some abuse,[11] and no such thing?

LAER. Know you the hand?

KING. 'Tis Hamlet's character.[12] 'Naked'—
And in a postscript here, he says 'Alone.'
Can you advise me?

LAER. I'm lost in it, my lord. But let him come.
It warms the very sickness in my heart
That I shall live and tell him to his teeth,
'Thus diest thou.'

KING. If it be so, Laertes—
As how should it be so, how otherwise?—
Will you be ruled by me?

LAER. Ay, my lord,
So you will not o'errule me to a peace.

KING. To thine own peace. If he be now return'd,
As checking at[13] his voyage, and that he means
No more to undertake it, I will work him
To an exploit now ripe in my device,
Under the which he shall not choose but fall;
And for his death no wind of blame shall breathe,
But even his mother shall uncharge[14] the practice,[15]
And call it accident.

LAER. My lord, I will be ruled;
The rather, if you could devise it so
That I might be the organ.

KING. It falls right.

[10] *naked*] destitute.
[11] *abuse*] deception.
[12] *character*] handwriting.
[13] *checking at*] turning from.
[14] *uncharge*] acquit of blame.
[15] *practice*] devious stratagem.

You have been talk'd of since your travel much,
And that in Hamlet's hearing, for a quality
Wherein, they say, you shine. Your sum of parts
Did not together pluck such envy from him,
As did that one, and that in my regard
Of the unworthiest siege.[16]

LAER. What part is that, my lord?

KING. A very ribbon in the cap of youth,
Yet needful too; for youth no less becomes
The light and careless livery that it wears
Than settled age his sables and his weeds,
Importing health and graveness. Two months since,
Here was a gentleman of Normandy—
I've seen myself, and served against, the French,
And they can well[17] on horseback; but this gallant
Had witchcraft in't. He grew unto his seat,
And to such wondrous doing brought his horse
As had he been incorpsed and demi-natured
With the brave beast. So far he topp'd my thought
That I, in forgery[18] of shapes and tricks,
Come short of what he did.

LAER. A Norman was't?

KING. A Norman.

LAER. Upon my life, Lamord.

KING. The very same.

LAER. I know him well. He is the brooch indeed
And gem of all the nation.

KING. He made confession of[19] you,
And gave you such a masterly report,
For art and exercise in your defence,[20]
And for your rapier most especial,
That he cried out, 'twould be a sight indeed
If one could match[21] you. The scrimers[22] of their nation,
He swore, had neither motion, guard, nor eye,
If you opposed them. Sir, this report of his

[16] *siege*] rank.
[17] *can well*] are skillful.
[18] *forgery*] invention.
[19] *made confession of*] spoke of.
[20] *defence*] swordmanship.
[21] *match*] engage in a match with.
[22] *scrimers*] fencers.

Did Hamlet so envenom with his envy
That he could nothing do but wish and beg
Your sudden coming o'er, to play with him.
Now, out of this—

LAER. What out of this, my lord?

KING. Laertes, was your father dear to you?
Or are you like the painting of a sorrow,
A face without a heart?

LAER. Why ask you this?

KING. Not that I think you did not love your father,
But that I know love is begun by time,
And that I see, in passages of proof,[23]
Time qualifies[24] the spark and fire of it.
There lives within the very flame of love
A kind of wick or snuff that will abate it;
And nothing is at a like goodness still,[25]
For goodness, growing to a pleurisy,
Dies in his own too much. That we would do,
We should do when we would; for this 'would' changes
And hath abatements and delays as many
As there are tongues, are hands, are accidents,
And then this 'should' is like a spendthrift sigh
That hurts by easing. But, to the quick o' the ulcer:
Hamlet comes back; what would you undertake
To show yourself your father's son in deed
More than in words?

LAER. To cut his throat i' the church.

KING. No place indeed should murder sanctuarize.[26]
Revenge should have no bounds. But, good Laertes,
Will you do this, keep close within your chamber.
Hamlet return'd shall know you are come home.
We'll put on[27] those shall praise your excellence
And set a double varnish on the fame
The Frenchman gave you, bring you in fine[28] together
And wager on your heads. He, being remiss,[29]
Most generous and free from all contriving,

[23] *passages of proof*] reliable instances.
[24] *qualifies*] diminishes.
[25] *still*] always.
[26] *sanctuarize*] give sanctuary to.
[27] *put on*] set to work.
[28] *in fine*] in the end.
[29] *remiss*] unsuspecting.

Will not peruse the foils, so that with ease,
Or with a little shuffling, you may choose
A sword unbated,[30] and in a pass[31] of practice
Requite him for your father.

LAER. I will do't.
And for that purpose I'll anoint my sword.
I bought an unction[32] of a mountebank,
So mortal that but dip a knife in it,
Where it draws blood no cataplasm[33] so rare,
Collected from all simples[34] that have virtue
Under the moon, can save the thing from death
That is but scratch'd withal. I'll touch my point
With this contagion that, if I gall[35] him slightly,
It may be death.

KING. Let's further think of this,
Weigh what convenience both of time and means
May fit us to our shape.[36] If this should fail,
And that our drift[37] look through our bad performance,
'Twere better not assay'd. Therefore this project
Should have a back or second that might hold
If this did blast in proof.[38] Soft, let me see.
We'll make a solemn wager on your cunnings—[39]
I ha't!
When in your motion you are hot and dry—
As make your bouts more violent to that end—
And that he calls for drink, I'll have prepared him
A chalice for the nonce; whereon but sipping,
If he by chance escape your venom'd stuck,[40]
Our purpose may hold there. But stay, what noise?

Enter QUEEN.

How now, sweet Queen?

QUEEN. One woe doth tread upon another's heel,

[30] *unbated*] unblunted (without a button on the point).
[31] *pass*] a single thrust or a bout.
[32] *unction*] ointment.
[33] *cataplasm*] plaster, poultice.
[34] *simples*] medicinal herbs.
[35] *gall*] wound.
[36] *shape*] form of proceeding.
[37] *drift*] scheme.
[38] *blast in proof*] fail when put to the test.
[39] *your cunnings*] your respective skill.
[40] *stuck*] thrust.

So fast they follow. Your sister's drown'd, Laertes.
LAER. Drown'd? O, where?
QUEEN. There is a willow grows aslant a brook,
That shows his hoary leaves in the glassy stream.
Therewith fantastic garlands did she make
Of crow-flowers,[41] nettles, daisies, and long purples,[42]
That liberal[43] shepherds give a grosser name,
But our cold[44] maids do dead men's fingers call them.
There, on the pendent boughs her crownet weeds
Clambering to hang, an envious[45] sliver broke;
When down her weedy trophies and herself
Fell in the weeping brook. Her clothes spread wide,
And mermaid-like awhile they bore her up;
Which time she chanted snatches of old lauds,[46]
As one incapable[47] of her own distress,
Or like a creature native and indued
Unto[48] that element. But long it could not be
Till that her garments, heavy with their drink,
Pull'd the poor wretch from her melodious lay
To muddy death.
LAER. Alas, then she is drown'd.
QUEEN. Drown'd, drown'd.
LAER. Too much of water hast thou, poor Ophelia,
And therefore I forbid my tears. But yet
It is our trick;[49] nature her custom holds,
Let shame say what it will. When these are gone,
The woman will be out.[50] Adieu, my lord.
I have a speech of fire that fain would blaze,
But that this folly douts it.[51] [*Exit.*
KING. Let's follow, Gertrude.
How much I had to do to calm his rage.
Now fear I this will give it start again;
Therefore let's follow. [*Exeunt.*

[41] *crow-flowers*] ragged robins.
[42] *long purples*] *Orchis mascula.*
[43] *liberal*] licentious.
[44] *cold*] chaste.
[45] *envious*] spiteful.
[46] *lauds*] hymns.
[47] *incapable*] unaware.
[48] *indued Unto*] suited to live in.
[49] *our trick*] in our nature.
[50] *When . . . out*] i.e., when I have shed these tears the woman in me will have been cast off, too.
[51] *this folly douts it*] this weeping extinguishes it.

ACT V.

SCENE I. *A churchyard.*

Enter two Clowns, *with spades, &c.*

FIRST CLO. Is she to be buried in Christian burial that wilfully seeks her own salvation?[1]

SEC. CLO. I tell thee she is; and therefore make her grave straight.[2] The crowner[3] hath sat on her, and finds it Christian burial.

FIRST CLO. How can that be, unless she drowned herself in her own defence?

SEC. CLO. Why, 'tis found so.

FIRST CLO. It must be *se offendendo*;[4] it cannot be else. For here lies the point: if I drown myself wittingly, it argues an act, and an act hath three branches: it is to act, to do, and to perform; argal,[5] she drowned herself wittingly.

SEC. CLO. Nay, but hear you, Goodman Delver—

FIRST CLO. Give me leave. Here lies the water—good. Here stands the man—good. If the man go to this water and drown himself, it is, will he, nill he, he goes. Mark you that. But if the water come to him and drown him, he drowns not himself; argal, he that is not guilty of his own death shortens not his own life.

SEC. CLO. But is this law?

FIRST CLO. Ay, marry, is't; crowner's quest[6] law.

[1] *Christian burial . . . salvation*] The Clowns assume that Ophelia has committed suicide and that therefore she cannot be buried in consecrated ground. *Salvation* is a blunder for "damnation."

[2] *straight*] straightaway.

[3] *crowner*] coroner.

[4] *se offendendo*] a blunder for *se defendendo* (in self-defense).

[5] *argal*] an uneducated pronunciation of "ergo."

[6] *quest*] inquest.

SEC. CLO. Will you ha' the truth on't? If this had not been a gentlewoman, she should have been buried out o' Christian burial.

FIRST CLO. Why, there thou say'st. And the more pity that great folk should have countenance in this world to drown or hang themselves, more than their even[7] Christian. Come, my spade. There is no ancient gentlemen but gardeners, ditchers and grave-makers: they hold up[8] Adam's profession.

SEC. CLO. Was he a gentleman?

FIRST CLO. A was the first that ever bore arms.

SEC. CLO. Why, he had none.

FIRST CLO. What, art a heathen? How dost thou understand the Scripture? The Scripture says Adam digged. Could he dig without arms? I'll put another question to thee. If thou answerest me not to the purpose, confess thyself—

SEC. CLO. Go to.

FIRST CLO. What is he that builds stronger than either the mason, the shipwright, or the carpenter?

SEC. CLO. The gallows-maker; for that frame outlives a thousand tenants.

FIRST CLO. I like thy wit well, in good faith. The gallows does well. But how does it well? It does well to those that do ill. Now, thou dost ill to say the gallows is built stronger than the church; argal, the gallows may do well to thee. To't again, come.

SEC. CLO. 'Who builds stronger than a mason, a shipwright, or a carpenter?'

FIRST CLO. Ay, tell me that, and unyoke.[9]

SEC. CLO. Marry, now I can tell.

FIRST CLO. To't.

SEC. CLO. Mass, I cannot tell.

Enter HAMLET *and* HORATIO, *afar off.*

FIRST CLO. Cudgel thy brains no more about it, for your dull ass will not mend his pace with beating, and when you are asked this question next, say 'A grave-maker.' The houses that he makes last till doomsday. Go, get thee to Yaughan. Fetch me a stoup of liquor.

[*Exit* Sec. Clown; First Clown *digs, and sings.*

[7] *even*] fellow.
[8] *hold up*] continue.
[9] *unyoke*] i.e., then your work is done.

In youth, when I did love, did love,
Methought it was very sweet,
To contract,[10] O, the time, for-a my behove,[11]
O, methought, there-a was nothing-a meet.

HAM. Has this fellow no feeling of his business, that he sings at grave-making?

HOR. Custom hath made it in him a property of easiness.[12]

HAM. 'Tis e'en so. The hand of little employment hath the daintier sense.

FIRST CLO. [*Sings*] But age, with his stealing steps,
Hath claw'd me in his clutch,
And hath shipped me intil[13] the land,
As if I had never been such. [*Throws up a skull.*]

HAM. That skull had a tongue in it, and could sing once. How the knave jowls[14] it to the ground, as if it were Cain's jawbone, that did the first murder. It might be the pate of a politician, which this ass now o'er-offices,[15] one that would circumvent God, might it not?

HOR. It might, my lord.

HAM. Or of a courtier, which could say 'Good morrow, sweet lord. How dost thou, sweet lord?' This might be my Lord Such-a-one, that praised my Lord Such-a-one's horse, when he meant to beg it, might it not?

HOR. Ay, my lord.

HAM. Why, e'en so; and now my Lady Worm's, chapless,[16] and knocked about the mazard[17] with a sexton's spade. Here's fine revolution, an we had the trick[18] to see't. Did these bones cost no more the breeding, but to play at loggats[19] with 'em? Mine ache to think on't.

FIRST CLO. [*Sings*] A pickaxe, and a spade, a spade,
For and[20] a shrouding-sheet;
O, a pit of clay for to be made
For such a guest is meet. [*Throws up another skull.*]

[10] *contract*] shorten (probably a blunder by the Clown).
[11] *behove*] behoof, advantage.
[12] *property of easiness*] activity that does not trouble the mind.
[13] *intil*] to.
[14] *jowls*] throws, dashes.
[15] *o'er-offices*] lords over (by virtue of his office as grave digger).
[16] *chapless*] without a jaw.
[17] *mazard*] head.
[18] *trick*] knack, art.
[19] *loggats*] a game in which small logs are thrown at a stake.
[20] *For and*] and moreover.

HAM. There's another. Why may not that be the skull of a lawyer? Where be his quiddities now, his quillets,[21] his cases, his tenures, and his tricks? Why does he suffer this rude knave now to knock him about the sconce with a dirty shovel, and will not tell him of his action of battery? Hum! This fellow might be in's time a great buyer of land, with his statutes, his recognizances, his fines, his double vouchers, his recoveries.[22] Is this the fine[23] of his fines and the recovery of his recoveries, to have his fine pate full of fine dirt? Will his vouchers vouch[24] him no more of his purchases, and double ones too, than the length and breadth of a pair of indentures?[25] The very conveyances of his lands will hardly lie in this box;[26] and must the inheritor[27] himself have no more, ha?

HOR. Not a jot more, my lord.

HAM. Is not parchment made of sheepskins?

HOR. Ay, my lord, and of calfskins too.

HAM. They are sheep and calves which seek out assurance in that. I will speak to this fellow. Whose grave's this, sirrah?

FIRST CLO. Mine, sir.

[*Sings*] O, a pit of clay for to be made
For such a guest is meet.

HAM. I think it be thine indeed, for thou liest in't.

FIRST CLO. You lie out on't, sir, and therefore 'tis not yours. For my part, I do not lie in't, and yet it is mine.

HAM. Thou dost lie in't, to be in't and say 'tis thine. 'Tis for the dead, not for the quick; therefore thou liest.

FIRST CLO. 'Tis a quick lie, sir; 'twill away again from me to you.

HAM. What man dost thou dig it for?

FIRST CLO. For no man, sir.

HAM. What woman then?

FIRST CLO. For none, neither.

HAM. Who is to be buried in't?

FIRST CLO. One that was a woman, sir, but, rest her soul, she's dead.

[21] *quiddities . . . quillets*] subtle arguments.

[22] *statutes . . . recoveries*] legal terms relating to the transfer and mortgaging of land.

[23] *fine*] end.

[24] *vouch*] guarantee.

[25] *indentures*] contracts.

[26] *box*] coffin.

[27] *inheritor*] possessor, owner.

HAM. How absolute[28] the knave is! We must speak by the card,[29] or equivocation will undo us. By the Lord, Horatio, this three years I have taken note of it: the age is grown so picked[30] that the toe of the peasant comes so near the heel of the courtier, he galls his kibe.[31] How long hast thou been a grave-maker?

FIRST CLO. Of all the days i' the year, I came to't that day that our last King Hamlet o'ercame Fortinbras.

HAM. How long is that since?

FIRST CLO. Cannot you tell that? Every fool can tell that. It was that very day that young Hamlet was born—he that is mad and sent into England.

HAM. Ay, marry, why was he sent into England?

FIRST CLO. Why, because a was mad. A shall recover his wits there; or, if a do not, 'tis no great matter there.

HAM. Why?

FIRST CLO. 'Twill not be seen in him there. There the men are as mad as he.

HAM. How came he mad?

FIRST CLO. Very strangely, they say.

HAM. How 'strangely'?

FIRST CLO. Faith, e'en with losing his wits.

HAM. Upon what ground?

FIRST CLO. Why, here in Denmark. I have been sexton here, man and boy, thirty years.

HAM. How long will a man lie i' the earth ere he rot?

FIRST CLO. I'faith, if a be not rotten before a die—as we have many pocky corses nowadays that will scarce hold the laying in[32]—a will last you some eight year or nine year. A tanner will last you nine year.

HAM. Why he more than another?

FIRST CLO. Why, sir, his hide is so tanned with his trade that a will keep out water a great while; and your water is a sore decayer of your whoreson dead body. Here's a skull, now. This skull has lain in the earth three and twenty years.

HAM. Whose was it?

FIRST CLO. A whoreson mad fellow's it was. Whose do you think it was?

[28] *absolute*] strict.
[29] *by the card*] with the utmost precision.
[30] *picked*] refined.
[31] *galls his kibe*] chafes the sore on his heel.
[32] *hold the laying in*] remain in one piece until after the burial.

HAM. Nay, I know not.

FIRST CLO. A pestilence on him for a mad rogue! A poured a flagon of Rhenish on my head once. This same skull, sir, was Yorick's skull, the King's jester.

HAM. [*Takes the skull*] This?

FIRST CLO. E'en that.

HAM. Alas, poor Yorick. I knew him, Horatio: a fellow of infinite jest, of most excellent fancy. He hath borne me on his back a thousand times; and now, how abhorred in my imagination it is! My gorge rises at it. Here hung those lips that I have kissed I know not how oft. Where be your gibes now, your gambols, your songs, your flashes of merriment, that were wont to set the table on a roar? Not one now to mock your own grinning? Quite chop-fallen? Now get you to my lady's chamber, and tell her, let her paint an inch thick, to this favour[33] she must come. Make her laugh at that. Prithee, Horatio, tell me one thing.

HOR. What's that, my lord?

HAM. Dost thou think Alexander looked o' this fashion i' the earth?

HOR. E'en so.

HAM. And smelt so? Pah! [*Puts down the skull.*

HOR. E'en so, my lord.

HAM. To what base uses we may return, Horatio! Why, may not imagination trace the noble dust of Alexander till he find it stopping a bung-hole?

HOR. 'Twere to consider too curiously[34] to consider so.

HAM. No, faith, not a jot; but to follow him thither with modesty[35] enough and likelihood to lead it, as thus: Alexander died, Alexander was buried, Alexander returneth into dust, the dust is earth, of earth we make loam, and why of that loam, whereto he was converted, might they not stop a beer-barrel?

Imperious[36] Cæsar, dead and turn'd to clay,
Might stop a hole to keep the wind away.
O, that that earth, which kept the world in awe,
Should patch a wall to expel the winter's flaw![37]
But soft, but soft awhile! Here comes the King,
The Queen, the courtiers.

[33] *favour*] appearance.
[34] *curiously*] minutely.
[35] *modestly*] moderation.
[36] *Imperious*] imperial.
[37] *flaw*] gust of wind.

Enter Priests, *&c. in procession; the Corpse of Ophelia,* LAERTES, *and* Mourners *following;* KING, QUEEN, *their trains, &c.*

Who is this they follow?
And with such maimed rites? This doth betoken
The corse they follow did with desperate hand
Fordo[38] its own life. 'Twas of some estate.[39]
Couch we[40] awhile and mark. [*Retiring with* HORATIO.

LAER. What ceremony else?

HAM. That is Laertes, a very noble youth. Mark.

LAER. What ceremony else?

PRIEST. Her obsequies have been as far enlarged
As we have warranty. Her death was doubtful;
And, but that great command o'ersways the order,
She should in ground unsanctified have lodged
Till the last trumpet; for charitable prayers,
Shards,[41] flints and pebbles should be thrown on her.
Yet here she is allow'd her virgin crants,[42]
Her maiden strewments[43] and the bringing home
Of bell and burial.[44]

LAER. Must there no more be done?

PRIEST. No more be done.
We should profane the service of the dead
To sing a requiem and such rest to her
As to peace-parted souls.

LAER. Lay her i' the earth,
And from her fair and unpolluted flesh
May violets spring. I tell thee, churlish priest,
A ministering angel shall my sister be
When thou liest howling.

HAM. What, the fair Ophelia!

QUEEN. [*Scattering flowers*] Sweets to the sweet. Farewell.
I hoped thou shouldst have been my Hamlet's wife;
I thought thy bride-bed to have deck'd, sweet maid,
And not have strew'd thy grave.

LAER. O, treble woe

[38] *Fordo*] destroy.
[39] *estate*] rank.
[40] *Couch we*] let us remain hidden.
[41] *Shards*] fragments of pottery.
[42] *crants*] garlands.
[43] *strewments*] strewing of flowers.
[44] *bringing home . . . burial*] laying to rest to the sound of the knell.

Fall ten times treble on that cursed head
Whose wicked deed thy most ingenious sense
Deprived thee of! Hold off the earth awhile,
Till I have caught her once more in mine arms.
[*Leaps into the grave.*
Now pile your dust upon the quick and dead,
Till of this flat a mountain you have made
To o'ertop old Pelion or the skyish head
Of blue Olympus.

HAM. [*Advancing*] What is he whose grief
Bears such an emphasis, whose phrase of sorrow
Conjures the wandering stars[45] and makes them stand
Like wonder-wounded hearers? This is I,
Hamlet the Dane.

LAER. The devil take thy soul! [*Grappling with him.*

HAM. Thou pray'st not well.
I prithee, take thy fingers from my throat;
For, though I am not splenative[46] and rash,
Yet have I in me something dangerous,
Which let thy wisdom fear. Hold off thy hand.

KING. Pluck them asunder.

QUEEN. Hamlet, Hamlet!

ALL. Gentlemen!

HOR. Good my lord, be quiet.

HAM. Why, I will fight with him upon this theme
Until my eyelids will no longer wag.

QUEEN. O my son, what theme?

HAM. I loved Ophelia. Forty thousand brothers
Could not, with all their quantity of love,
Make up my sum. What wilt thou do for her?

KING. O, he is mad, Laertes.

QUEEN. For love of God, forbear[47] him.

HAM. 'Swounds, show me what thou'lt do.
Woo't[48] weep, woo't fight, woo't fast, woo't tear thyself,
Woo't drink up eisel,[49] eat a crocodile?
I'll do't. Dost thou come here to whine,
To outface me with leaping in her grave?

[45] *wandering stars*] planets.
[46] *splenative*] hot-tempered, impetuous.
[47] *forbear*] leave alone.
[48] *Woo't*] will you.
[49] *eisel*] vinegar.

Be buried quick[50] with her, and so will I.
And, if thou prate of mountains, let them throw
Millions of acres on us, till our ground,
Singeing his pate against the burning zone,[51]
Make Ossa like a wart. Nay, an thou'lt mouth,
I'll rant as well as thou.

QUEEN. This is mere madness;
And thus awhile the fit will work on him.
Anon, as patient as the female dove
When that her golden couplets are disclosed,[52]
His silence will sit drooping.

HAM. Hear you, sir;
What is the reason that you use me thus?
I loved you ever. But it is no matter.
Let Hercules himself do what he may,
The cat will mew, and dog will have his day. [*Exit.*

KING. I pray thee, good Horatio, wait upon him. [*Exit* HORATIO.
[*To* LAERTES] Strengthen your patience in our last night's speech;
We'll put the matter to the present push.—[53]
Good Gertrude, set some watch over your son.
This grave shall have a living monument.
An hour of quiet shortly shall we see;
Till then, in patience our proceeding be. [*Exeunt.*

SCENE II. *A hall in the castle.*

Enter HAMLET *and* HORATIO.

HAM. So much for this, sir. Now shall you see the other.
You do remember all the circumstance?

HOR. Remember it, my lord!

HAM. Sir, in my heart there was a kind of fighting
That would not let me sleep. Methought I lay

[50] *quick*] alive.
[51] *burning zone*] sun's sphere or orbit.
[52] *disclosed*] hatched.
[53] *to the present push*] into immediate action.

Worse than the mutines in the bilboes.[1] Rashly—
And praised be rashness for it: let us know
Our indiscretion sometime serves us well
When our deep plots do pall; and that should learn us
There's a divinity that shapes our ends,
Rough-hew them how we will—

HOR. That is most certain.

HAM. Up from my cabin,
My sea-gown scarf'd about me, in the dark
Groped I to find out them,[2] had my desire,
Finger'd[3] their packet, and in fine[4] withdrew
To mine own room again, making so bold,
My fears forgetting manners, to unseal
Their grand commission, where I found, Horatio—
O royal knavery!—an exact command,
Larded[5] with many several sorts of reasons
Importing Denmark's health and England's too,
With, ho! such bugs and goblins in my life,[6]
That on the supervise,[7] no leisure bated,[8]
No, not to stay the grinding of the axe,
My head should be struck off.

HOR. Is't possible?

HAM. Here's the commission. Read it at more leisure.
But wilt thou hear now how I did proceed?

HOR. I beseech you.

HAM. Being thus benetted round with villanies—
Or[9] I could make a prologue to my brains,
They had begun the play—I sat me down,
Devised a new commission, wrote it fair.[10]
I once did hold it, as our statists[11] do,
A baseness to write fair, and labour'd much
How to forget that learning; but, sir, now
It did me yeoman's service. Wilt thou know

[1] *mutines in the bilboes*] mutineers in shackles.
[2] *them*] Rosencrantz and Guildenstern.
[3] *Finger'd*] pilfered.
[4] *in fine*] finally.
[5] *Larded*] garnished.
[6] *such bugs . . . life*] such imaginary dangers, should I be allowed to live.
[7] *supervise*] perusal (of Claudius' missive).
[8] *no leisure bated*] with no delay.
[9] *Or*] before.
[10] *fair*] in a legible hand.
[11] *statists*] statesmen.

The effect of what I wrote?
HOR. Ay, good my lord.
HAM. An earnest conjuration from the King,
As England was his faithful tributary,
As love between them like the palm might flourish,
As peace should still[12] her wheaten garland wear
And stand a comma 'tween their amities,
And many such-like 'As'es of great charge,[13]
That on the view and knowing of these contents,
Without debatement further, more or less,
He should the bearers put to sudden death,
Not shriving-time[14] allow'd.
HOR. How was this seal'd?
HAM. Why, even in that was heaven ordinant.[15]
I had my father's signet in my purse,
Which was the model of that Danish seal;
Folded the writ up in the form of the other,
Subscribed it, gave't the impression, placed it safely,
The changeling never known. Now, the next day
Was our sea-fight; and what to this was sequent
Thou know'st already.
HOR. So Guildenstern and Rosencrantz go to't.
HAM. Why, man, they did make love to this employment.
They are not near my conscience. Their defeat
Does by their own insinuation grow.
'Tis dangerous when the baser nature comes
Between the pass[16] and fell incensed points
Of mighty opposites.
HOR. Why, what a king is this!
HAM. Does it not, think thee, stand me now upon—[17]
He that hath kill'd my king and whored my mother,
Popp'd in between the election and my hopes,
Thrown out his angle[18] for my proper[19] life,
And with such cozenage[20]—is't not perfect conscience
To quit him with this arm? And is't not to be damn'd

[12] *still*] always.
[13] *charge*] importance. There is a pun on "asses," and the load they carry.
[14] *shriving-time*] time for absolution.
[15] *ordinant*] ordaining, directing.
[16] *pass*] sword thrust.
[17] *stand me now upon*] put me under obligation.
[18] *angle*] fishhook.
[19] *proper*] own.
[20] *cozenage*] deceit.

To let this canker of our nature come
In further evil?

HOR. It must be shortly known to him from England
What is the issue of the business there.

HAM. It will be short. The interim is mine;
And a man's life's no more than to say 'One.'
But I am very sorry, good Horatio,
That to Laertes I forgot myself;
For by the image of my cause I see
The portraiture of his. I'll court his favours.
But, sure, the bravery[21] of his grief did put me
Into a towering passion.

HOR. Peace, who comes here?

Enter OSRIC.

OSR. Your lordship is right welcome back to Denmark.

HAM. I humbly thank you, sir. Dost know this water-fly?

HOR. No, my good lord.

HAM. Thy state is the more gracious,[22] for 'tis a vice to know him. He hath much land, and fertile. Let a beast be lord of beasts, and his crib[23] shall stand at the king's mess. 'Tis a chuff,[24] but, as I say, spacious in the possession of dirt.

OSR. Sweet lord, if your lordship were at leisure, I should impart a thing to you from his Majesty.

HAM. I will receive it, sir, with all diligence of spirit. Put your bonnet to his right use: 'tis for the head.

OSR. I thank your lordship, it is very hot.

HAM. No, believe me, 'tis very cold; the wind is northerly.

OSR. It is indifferent[25] cold, my lord, indeed.

HAM. But yet methinks it is very sultry and hot for my complexion.[26]

OSR. Exceedingly, my lord. It is very sultry, as 'twere—I cannot tell how. But, my lord, his Majesty bade me signify to you that he has laid a great wager on your head. Sir, this is the matter—

HAM. I beseech you, remember—

[HAMLET *moves him to put on his hat.*

[21] *bravery*] bravado, ostentation.
[22] *gracious*] virtuous.
[23] *crib*] manger, trough.
[24] *chuff*] a wealthy, but dull, person.
[25] *indifferent*] moderately.
[26] *complexion*] temperament, constitution.

OSR. Nay, good my lord; for mine ease, in good faith. Sir, here is newly come to court Laertes—believe me, an absolute gentleman, full of most excellent differences,[27] of very soft society and great showing.[28] Indeed, to speak feelingly[29] of him, he is the card or calendar of gentry,[30] for you shall find in him the continent[31] of what part a gentleman would see.

HAM. Sir, his definement suffers no perdition[32] in you, though, I know, to divide him inventorially would dizzy the arithmetic of memory, and yet but yaw neither,[33] in respect of his quick sail. But, in the verity of extolment, I take him to be a soul of great article,[34] and his infusion[35] of such dearth[36] and rareness as, to make true diction of him, his semblable is his mirror,[37] and who else would trace[38] him, his umbrage,[39] nothing more.

OSR. Your lordship speaks most infallibly of him.

HAM. The concernancy,[40] sir? Why do we wrap the gentleman in our more rawer breath?[41]

OSR. Sir?

HOR. Is't not possible to understand in another tongue?[42] You will do't, sir, really.

HAM. What imports the nomination[43] of this gentleman?

OSR. Of Laertes?

HOR. His purse is empty already; all's golden words are spent.

HAM. Of him, sir.

OSR. I know you are not ignorant—

HAM. I would you did, sir. Yet, in faith, if you did, it would not much approve[44] me. Well, sir?

27 *differences*] extraordinary qualities.
28 *soft society . . . showing*] distinguished appearance.
29 *feelingly*] perceptively.
30 *card or calendar of gentry*] epitome of courtesy.
31 *continent*] container.
32 *perdition*] loss.
33 *but yaw neither*] steer out of course nevertheless.
34 *article*] i.e., matter to be listed on an inventory.
35 *infusion*] quality.
36 *dearth*] rarity.
37 *his semblable is his mirror*] the only person like him is his own reflection.
38 *trace*] follow.
39 *umbrage*] shadow.
40 *concernancy*] import, significance.
41 *more rawer breath*] inadequate language.
42 *another tongue*] i.e., simpler terms.
43 *nomination*] mentioning.
44 *approve*] commend.

OSR. You are not ignorant of what excellence Laertes is—

HAM. I dare not confess that, lest I should compare with him in excellence; but, to know a man well were to know himself.

OSR. I mean, sir, for his weapon; but in the imputation[45] laid on him by them in his meed,[46] he's unfellowed.

HAM. What's his weapon?

OSR. Rapier and dagger.

HAM. That's two of his weapons. But, well.

OSR. The King, sir, hath wagered with him six Barbary horses, against the which he has impawned,[47] as I take it, six French rapiers and poniards,[48] with their assigns,[49] as girdle, hanger,[50] and so. Three of the carriages, in faith, are very dear to fancy, very responsive[51] to the hilts, most delicate carriages, and of very liberal conceit.[52]

HAM. What call you the carriages?

HOR. I knew you must be edified by the margent[53] ere you had done.

OSR. The carriages, sir, are the hangers.

HAM. The phrase would be more german[54] to the matter if we could carry a cannon by our sides. I would it might be hangers till then. But, on. Six Barbary horses against six French swords, their assigns, and three liberal-conceited carriages—that's the French bet against the Danish. Why is this 'impawned,' as you call it?

OSR. The King, sir, hath laid, sir, that in a dozen passes[55] between yourself and him, he shall not exceed you three hits. He hath laid on twelve for nine. And it would come to immediate trial, if your lordship would vouchsafe the answer.

HAM. How if I answer no?

OSR. I mean, my lord, the opposition of your person in trial.

HAM. Sir, I will walk here in the hall. If it please his Majesty, it is the breathing time[56] of day with me. Let the foils be brought,

[45] *imputation*] reputation.
[46] *meed*] service.
[47] *impawned*] wagered.
[48] *poniards*] daggers.
[49] *assigns*] accessories.
[50] *hanger*] part of a belt to which the scabbard is attached.
[51] *responsive*] matching, suited.
[52] *liberal conceit*] (?) tasteful design.
[53] *margent*] margin (of a book, on which could be written explanatory notes).
[54] *german*] germane, appropriate.
[55] *passes*] bouts.
[56] *breathing time*] exercise period.

the gentleman willing, and the King hold his purpose, I will win for him an I can. If not, I will gain nothing but my shame and the odd hits.

OSR. Shall I redeliver you e'en so?

HAM. To this effect, sir, after what flourish your nature will.

OSR. I commend my duty to your lordship.

HAM. Yours, yours. [*Exit* OSRIC.] He does well to commend it himself; there are no tongues else for's turn.

HOR. This lapwing runs away with the shell on his head.[57]

HAM. He did comply with his dug[58] before he sucked it. Thus has he—and many more of the same breed that I know the drossy[59] age dotes on—only got the tune of the time and outward habit of encounter, a kind of yesty[60] collection, which carries them through and through the most fanned and winnowed[61] opinions; and do but blow them to their trial, the bubbles are out.[62]

Enter a Lord.

LORD. My lord, his Majesty commended him to you by young Osric, who brings back to him that you attend him in the hall. He sends to know if your pleasure hold to play with Laertes or that you will take longer time.

HAM. I am constant to my purposes; they follow the King's pleasure. If his fitness[63] speaks, mine is ready; now or whensoever, provided I be so able as now.

LORD. The King and Queen and all are coming down.

HAM. In happy time.

LORD. The Queen desires you to use some gentle entertainment[64] to Laertes before you fall to play.

HAM. She well instructs me. [*Exit* Lord.

HOR. You will lose this wager, my lord.

HAM. I do not think so. Since he went into France, I have been in

[57] *This lapwing . . . head*] Horatio refers to the fact that Osric has put his hat back on. Lapwings were said to leave the nest shortly after hatching and therefore came to signify precocity and pretension.

[58] *did comply . . . dug*] was courteous to his mother's breast.

[59] *drossy*] frivolous.

[60] *yesty*] frothy.

[61] *fanned and winnowed*] tried and sifted.

[62] *do but blow . . . out*] i.e., when you put them to the test by conversing with them their expressions are found to be empty.

[63] *fitness*] convenience.

[64] *gentle entertainment*] courtesy.

continual practice. I shall win at the odds. But thou wouldst not think how ill all's here about my heart; but it is no matter.

HOR. Nay, good my lord—

HAM. It is but foolery; but it is such a kind of gain-giving[65] as would perhaps trouble a woman.

HOR. If your mind dislike anything, obey it. I will forestall their repair hither and say you are not fit.

HAM. Not a whit. We defy augury. There is special providence in the fall of a sparrow. If it be now, 'tis not to come; if it be not to come, it will be now; if it be not now, yet it will come. The readiness is all. Since no man has aught of what he leaves, what is't to leave betimes? Let be.

Enter KING, QUEEN, LAERTES, *and* Lords, OSRIC *and other* Attendants *with foils and gauntlets; a table and flagons of wine on it.*

KING. Come, Hamlet, come, and take this hand from me.
[*The* KING *puts* LAERTES' *hand into* HAMLET's.

HAM. Give me your pardon, sir. I've done you wrong;
But pardon't as you are a gentleman.
This presence[66] knows,
And you must needs have heard, how I am punish'd
With sore distraction. What I have done
That might your nature, honour and exception[67]
Roughly awake, I here proclaim was madness.
Was't Hamlet wrong'd Laertes? Never Hamlet.
If Hamlet from himself be ta'en away,
And when he's not himself does wrong Laertes,
Then Hamlet does it not, Hamlet denies it.
Who does it then? His madness. If't be so,
Hamlet is of the faction that is wrong'd;
His madness is poor Hamlet's enemy.
Sir, in this audience,
Let my disclaiming from a purposed evil
Free me so far in your most generous thoughts
That I have shot mine arrow o'er the house
And hurt my brother.

LAER. I am satisfied in nature,
Whose motive in this case should stir me most
To my revenge; but in my terms of honour

[65] *gain-giving*] misgiving.
[66] *presence*] noble assembly.
[67] *exception*] disapproval.

I stand aloof, and will no reconcilement
Till by some elder masters of known honour
I have a voice[68] and precedent of peace
To keep my name ungored. But till that time
I do receive your offer'd love like love
And will not wrong it.

HAM. I embrace it freely,
And will this brother's wager frankly play.—
Give us the foils. Come on.

LAER. Come, one for me.

HAM. I'll be your foil,[69] Laertes. In mine ignorance
Your skill shall, like a star i' the darkest night,
Stick fiery off[70] indeed.

LAER. You mock me, sir.

HAM. No, by this hand.

KING. Give them the foils, young Osric. Cousin Hamlet,
You know the wager?

HAM. Very well, my lord.
Your Grace has laid the odds o' the weaker side.

KING. I do not fear it; I have seen you both,
But since he is better'd, we have therefore odds.

LAER. This is too heavy; let me see another.

HAM. This likes me well. These foils have all a length?
[*They prepare to play.*

OSR. Ay, my good lord.

KING. Set me the stoups of wine upon that table.
If Hamlet give the first or second hit,
Or quit in answer of the third exchange,
Let all the battlements their ordnance fire:
The King shall drink to Hamlet's better breath,
And in the cup an union[71] shall he throw,
Richer than that which four successive kings
In Denmark's crown have worn. Give me the cups;
And let the kettle to the trumpet speak,
The trumpet to the cannoneer without,
The cannons to the heavens, the heaven to earth,
'Now the King drinks to Hamlet.' Come, begin.
And you, the judges, bear a wary eye.

[68] *voice*] authoritative judgment.
[69] *foil*] background on which a jewel is placed.
[70] *Stick fiery off*] stand out brightly.
[71] *union*] pearl.

HAM. Come on, sir.
LAER. Come, my lord. [*They play.*
HAM. One.
LAER. No.
HAM. Judgement.
OSR. A hit, a very palpable hit.
LAER. Well, again.
KING. Stay; give me drink. Hamlet, this pearl is thine.
Here's to thy health.
[*Trumpets sound, and cannon shot off within.*
Give him the cup.
HAM. I'll play this bout first. Set it by awhile.
Come. [*They play.*] Another hit. What say you?
LAER. A touch, a touch, I do confess.
KING. Our son shall win.
QUEEN. He's fat[72] and scant of breath.
Here, Hamlet, take my napkin, rub thy brows.
The Queen carouses to thy fortune, Hamlet.
HAM. Good madam.
KING. Gertrude, do not drink.
QUEEN. I will, my lord; I pray you, pardon me.
KING. [*Aside*] It is the poison'd cup; it is too late.
HAM. I dare not drink yet, madam—by and by.
QUEEN. Come, let me wipe thy face.
LAER. My lord, I'll hit him now.
KING. I do not think't.
LAER. [*Aside*] And yet it is almost against my conscience.
HAM. Come, for the third, Laertes. You but dally.
I pray you, pass[73] with your best violence.
I am afeard you make a wanton of me.[74]
LAER. Say you so? Come on. [*They play.*
OSR. Nothing, neither way.
LAER. Have at you now!
[*Laertes wounds* HAMLET; *then, in scuffling, they change rapiers, and* HAMLET *wounds* LAERTES.
KING. Part them; they are incensed.
HAM. Nay, come, again. [*The* QUEEN *falls.*
OSR. Look to the Queen there, ho!
HOR. They bleed on both sides. How is it, my lord?

[72] *fat*] unfit.
[73] *pass*] thrust.
[74] *make a wanton of me*] treat me like a spoiled child.

OSR. How is't, Laertes?
LAER. Why, as a woodcock to mine own springe,[75] Osric.
I am justly kill'd with mine own treachery.
HAM. How does the Queen?
KING. She swoons to see them bleed.
QUEEN. No, no, the drink, the drink—O my dear Hamlet—
The drink, the drink! I am poison'd. [*Dies.*
HAM. O villany! Ho! Let the door be lock'd.
Treachery! Seek it out. [*Exit* OSRIC; LAERTES *falls.*
LAER. It is here, Hamlet. Hamlet, thou art slain.
No medicine in the world can do thee good;
In thee there is not half an hour of life.
The treacherous instrument is in thy hand,
Unbated and envenom'd. The foul practice[76]
Hath turn'd itself on me. Lo, here I lie,
Never to rise again. Thy mother's poison'd.
I can no more. The King, the King's to blame.
HAM. The point envenom'd too? Then, venom, to thy work.
[*Stabs the* KING.
ALL. Treason! treason!
KING. O, yet defend me, friends. I am but hurt.
HAM. Here, thou incestuous, murderous, damned Dane,
Drink off this potion. Is thy union here?
Follow my mother. [KING *dies.*
LAER. He is justly served.
It is a poison temper'd[77] by himself.
Exchange forgiveness with me, noble Hamlet.
Mine and my father's death come not upon thee,
Nor thine on me. [*Dies.*
HAM. Heaven make thee free of it. I follow thee.
I am dead, Horatio. Wretched[78] Queen, adieu!
You that look pale and tremble at this chance,
That are but mutes or audience to this act,
Had I but time—as this fell sergeant,[79] Death,
Is strict in his arrest—O, I could tell you—
But let it be. Horatio, I am dead,
Thou livest. Report me and my cause aright

[75] *springe*] snare.
[76] *practice*] strategem, insidious device.
[77] *temper'd*] mixed.
[78] *Wretched*] unhappy.
[79] *sergeant*] sheriff's officer.

To the unsatisfied.
HOR. Never believe it.
I am more an antique Roman[80] than a Dane.
Here's yet some liquor left.
HAM. As thou'rt a man,
Give me the cup. Let go. By heaven, I'll have't.
O God, Horatio, what a wounded name,
Things standing thus unknown, shall live behind me!
If thou didst ever hold me in thy heart,
Absent thee from felicity awhile,
And in this harsh world draw thy breath in pain
To tell my story. [*March afar off, and shot within.*

Enter OSRIC.

What warlike noise is this?
OSR. Young Fortinbras, with conquest come from Poland,
To the ambassadors of England gives
This warlike volley.
HAM. O, I die, Horatio.
The potent poison quite o'er-crows[81] my spirit.
I cannot live to hear the news from England;
But I do prophesy the election lights
On Fortinbras. He has my dying voice.
So tell him, with the occurrents,[82] more and less,
Which have solicited.[83] The rest is silence. [*Dies.*
HOR. Now cracks a noble heart. Good night, sweet prince,
And flights of angels sing thee to thy rest. [*March within.*
Why does the drum come hither?

Enter FORTINBRAS, *and the* English Ambassadors, *with drum, colours, and* Attendants.

FORT. Where is this sight?
HOR. What is it you would see?
If aught of woe or wonder,[84] cease your search.
FORT. This quarry cries on havoc.[85] O proud Death,
What feast is toward in thine eternal cell,
That thou so many princes at a shot

[80] *antique Roman*] i.e., one who chooses suicide rather than a dishonorable life.
[81] *o'er-crows*] triumphs over.
[82] *occurrents*] occurrences.
[83] *solicited*] moved (me to choose him).
[84] *wonder*] destruction, grief.
[85] *This quarry cries on havoc*] This heap of dead proclaims indiscriminate slaughter.

So bloodily hast struck?

FIRST AMB. The sight is dismal;[86]
And our affairs from England come too late.
The ears are senseless that should give us hearing
To tell him his commandment is fulfill'd,
That Rosencrantz and Guildenstern are dead.
Where should we have our thanks?

HOR. Not from his mouth,
Had it the ability of life to thank you.
He never gave commandment for their death.
But since so jump upon this bloody question[87]
You from the Polack wars, and you from England,
Are here arrived, give order that these bodies
High on a stage[88] be placed to the view;
And let me speak to the yet unknowing world
How these things came about. So shall you hear
Of carnal, bloody and unnatural acts,
Of accidental judgements, casual[89] slaughters,
Of deaths put on[90] by cunning and forced[91] cause,
And, in this upshot, purposes mistook
Fall'n on the inventors' heads. All this can I
Truly deliver.

FORT. Let us haste to hear it,
And call the noblest to the audience.
For me, with sorrow I embrace my fortune.
I have some rights of memory[92] in this kingdom,
Which now to claim my vantage doth invite me.

HOR. Of that I shall have also cause to speak,
And from his mouth whose voice will draw on more.[93]
But let this same[94] be presently perform'd,
Even while men's minds are wild, lest more mischance
On[95] plots and errors happen.

FORT. Let four captains
Bear Hamlet like a soldier to the stage;

[86] *dismal*] horrifying.
[87] *jump . . . question*] immediately after this bloody business.
[88] *stage*] platform.
[89] *casual*] accidental.
[90] *put on*] instigated.
[91] *forced*] violent.
[92] *of memory*] traditional, remembered.
[93] *draw on more*] influence others (to vote for Fortinbras).
[94] *this same*] the aforementioned.
[95] *On*] in addition to; (?) as a result of.

For he was likely, had he been put on,
To have proved most royal; and, for his passage,[96]
The soldiers' music and the rites of war
Speak loudly for him.
Take up the bodies. Such a sight as this
Becomes the field, but here shows much amiss.
Go, bid the soldiers shoot.

[A *dead march. Exeunt, bearing off the bodies; after which a peal of ordnance is shot off.*

[96] *passage*] passing, death.